Love Like This

United Faedom Publishing

ISBN: 9798829350604

United Faedom Publishing

Anthologies

Untamed
Tot Tales
Merrow
Nevermore
Nightshade and Moonlight
Songs of the Rainbow (poetry)
Cozy Kisses
Pride and Passion (LGBTQ+)

Author Collections

Fiction Kingdom by Jensen Reed
Tales from the World Next Door by Joshua D. Taylor
Diverse Shadows by Melissa Sell

Novels and Novellas

The Chronicles of Fey, Rising, by Melissa Sell

Contents

Brandy

Donise Sheppard

Brandy wiped away her tears and looked out over the horizon. Since moving to Shetland, she'd come out to sit near the edge of the cliff and watch the sun set over the ocean. Everything here was so beautiful and peaceful. It was just her and her thoughts and the ebb and flow of the waves on the beach below.

She didn't anticipate how lonely she would be, leaving all her friends and family behind in America, especially now that it was the holidays. Nobody here was celebrating Thanksgiving, but she would have loved to cook a meal for a few friends if only she had any. She got along with a few of the locals. They were friendly enough, but they weren't friends. They'd never asked Brandy to go out or stop by for a visit.

Brandy had asked one man on a date, but he said he'd just gotten out of a relationship and wasn't looking for anything serious. He was still interested in going out, but Brandy didn't want a fling. She'd left that Brandy back in America.

She was looking for something more serious, something stable and long-term. That's why she moved to a small town and bought the best house she could afford.

Her house was everything she wanted. The gray stone brick gave it the appearance of an old castle. There was a living room, dining room, kitchen, and a study where she could work. She bought a four-bedroom, three-bath, with hopes of meeting a nice man and starting a family, but so far, it's just been her in the big house.

She sniffled and brushed away fresh tears.

She was starting to wonder how she ever expected to meet someone in such a small town, where nobody knew her or seemed to want to know her. Perhaps she'd be alone here forever. Maybe she should have bought the one-bedroom cottage for sale down the road.

She could always sell her beautiful home and move back to Florida. Her sister, Sarah, had asked her to come home several times, but Brandy always told her she was happy where she was. And she was, for the most part. It was just the feeling of being so completely alone and isolated that made her question the move.

If she would get a job somewhere rather than work from home, she might do better. Maybe she'd even meet a few friends and a nice guy. But where was she going to work in Shetland with a degree in creative writing?

You can always come home.

Truth was, she didn't want to move back. There were too many people, it was always so hot, and she was almost as lonely there as she was in Scotland. At least now she had a house she loved.

The sun was sinking lower. Brandy wrapped her sweater around herself tighter. She loved how cool the temperature was here in the summer, but the late fall was proving to be too chilly for comfort. She was dreading how cold the winter would be. Still, it was bound to be better than Florida's summer heat.

She picked up her mug, now empty of tea, and made her way up the backyard, toward the house. She had just stepped onto the concrete patio when she saw a man, dressed in shorts but no shirt, walking up the hill from the beach toward her. He was muscular, with at least a four-pack. His wavy, dark brown hair was wet as if he'd just gone swimming.

But it was too cold for swimming. Only someone crazy would want to swim in Shetland in November.

She lived almost a mile from anyone else, but it crossed her mind that perhaps he had gone swimming and got lost. Maybe the tide carried him away from where he went in. He might need a towel and a phone to call for a ride.

Brandy shivered and set her mug on the patio table. She suddenly wished the sun was higher in the sky so she could see him better, but all she had was a myriad of oranges and pinks.

"Can I help you?" she called. Her voice carried in the still, late evening.

As soon as the man saw her, he smiled. Brandy's heart raced. Sure, he was devilishly handsome, but she didn't know him. She lived alone.

He walked to the edge of her property and stopped. He stood at least a head taller than Brandy and was even more handsome up close. He was around her age, maybe a little older, she guessed twenty-five to thirty, with bright blue eyes and freckles across his cheeks and nose.

"Sorry ta bother you, but I saw ya cryin' and I wanted ta check and see if I could help you." His accent was thick, but he didn't talk as fast as some of the locals, so Brandy had no trouble understanding him.

Brandy narrowed her eyes. "You saw me crying? How?"

"I was swimming. Looked up and saw ya."

"Oh. You must have good eyesight."

"Well, they work for me. That's what matters, right?"

Brandy laughed and looked at her feet. "I suppose. I'm alright, though, thank you. Just a little homesick."

"I'm glad ta hear it. Not the homesick part, just … well, you know." He gave her another smile before looking out at the sea. "I'll go now. Let you get on with it." But he didn't move. He seemed content with just standing in the cool breeze, looking at Brandy.

"Do you want a towel?" she asked. "I can get you one. And a cup of tea to warm you?"

He eyed her for a moment, then looked back toward the hill.

"Well, alright. I suppose I could stay for a cuppa."

"Good." Brandy could hardly hide her excitement. "You can have a seat, somewhere out here," she motioned at the patio chairs, the swing in the yard, and the two chairs beside the cliff, overlooking the ocean, "if you want. I'll be out in a minute. I'm Brandy, by the way."

"It's lovely to meet you, Brandy. I'm Rory."

"It's nice to meet you too, Rory. Have a seat if you like. I'll be right out."

She was being reckless, she knew she was, but he was so cute and seemed like an alright guy so far. He was funny. He didn't try to come too close until she gave him permission. That was a good sign, right?

She started the teapot, then fetched a towel for Rory. On her way back to the kitchen, she grabbed a blanket from the hall closet for him to use to keep warm. She glanced out the glass sliding door and saw him sitting on the swing, overlooking the pond and flower garden. He looked comfortable. When he looked toward the house, he waved at Brandy, who smiled and waved back.

Brandy set two steaming mugs of tea on a tray, along with sugar, milk, and a bag of cookies, threw the towel and blanket over her arm and made her way to the garden. Rory stood as she approached.

"I didn't know if you like milk or sugar, but I brought both."

"Thank you. That's really kind."

Brandy handed him the towel, and he patted his chest and arms, tousling his hair.

"Um …" She quickly sat down, blushing as she realized she'd been staring. How long had it been since she'd seen a man this close without a shirt? It had been at least six months, and he wasn't half as attractive as Rory. "So, do you live around here, or are you just visiting?"

He smiled, showing a perfect row of teeth. "I live pretty close to here." He wrapped the blanket around himself and sat back down.

"It's a beautiful place to live."

"Tis. You aren't from around here, though. Are you visitin' someone? A boyfriend, perhaps?"

Brandy bit her lip as a smile spread across her face. He seemed to be interested in her as well. "No. I'm here to stay, and I don't have a boyfriend. I came here a few years ago with my dad. His great grandparents came from here. I absolutely fell in love with it, so I saved up and moved."

"Did your da come with you?"

"Oh, no. He – uh … died two years ago."

"I'm sorry to hear that." He looked at her for a moment before taking a sip of tea. "What about your mum?"

Brandy shook her head and stared at her steaming mug. "She died when I was four. I never really knew her, but Dad loved her more than anything. He never remarried. It's just me and my sister, Sarah, now. And her husband and two kids."

“That’s a shame. I’m glad you have a sister, though. My parents died a couple years back. There was a …” he hesitated, “… fishing accident. I never had any siblings.”

There she was, crying about being lonely, and he was completely alone, without family at all. At least she’d been blessed with a sister, niece, and nephew.

“I’m sorry.”

“Thank you.”

“So, what were you doing swimming? It’s freezing out here.”

He chuckled. “It’s not so bad. I feel better in the cold water than I do on land, with the biting wind. The ocean is home.”

He was a sailor? He must be used to the cold wind. Still, being soaking wet and swimming in the middle of November couldn’t be fun or smart, for that matter.

“Well, still. You should be careful. You don’t want to catch a cold.”

“I will. Where did you grow up?” he asked, not taking his eyes off hers. They were kind and the deepest blue she’d ever seen. Was there anything about him that wasn’t attractive?

“America. Florida. It stays hot there all year round. It’s taking me a while to adjust to the cold, but I’m determined to do it.”

“You didn’t like the heat?”

Brandy laughed. “No. That’s one thing I won’t miss at all.”

They talked for another hour in the dark garden, with only the light from the porch and moonlight. Rory seemed more than comfortable, sitting, and chatting in the cold, and as long as he wanted to talk, Brady wasn’t going to stop him. She thought about inviting him inside, but she was nervous. She’d just met him. Eventually, as the night went on, Brandy got so cold her teeth began to chatter.

“Here, have the blanket,” Rory said, standing up and holding it out. His bare chest was once again exposed to the wind. Brandy inhaled and bit her lip. She had already forgotten how hot he was.

“No! You need it. You aren’t even wearing a shirt.”

Rory looked down and grinned. “Right. Perhaps I should go and let you get inside, then. It’s getting late.”

Brandy's heart sank. She wasn't ready for him to leave. This was the longest conversation she'd had in months. It didn't hurt that he was cute and interesting and seemed to like her.

But she didn't want to invite him inside and have him assume she wanted to have sex. It didn't matter how hot Rory was.

However, it was getting too cold for comfort, and maybe he was just as cold as she was but too polite to say so. She had no right to ask him to stay, especially with him dressed the way he was.

"Alright. Well … it was nice to meet you, and to chat for a bit."

"And you, Brandy. Perhaps, if you aren't busy, we can have tea again soon."

Brandy smiled, a sudden warmth spreading through her. She wanted to ask him out but didn't have the nerve. He just saved her from the regret she would've had if she'd let him walk away.

"That would be great. Should I give you my number?"

Rory cocked his head and studied her. "Are you busy tomorrow night?"

"Nope." She shrugged. "Not busy at all."

"Then I'll be here. If that's alright with you."

Brandy smiled. "That sounds good. What time should I expect you? I can make dinner, er tea, if you'd like."

"Dinner would be lovely. I can be here about the same time I was today. After the sun goes down."

"Work the day away, huh?"

"Gotta earn my keep." He stood and held out the blanket.

"You can hang onto that. It's gotten pretty chilly."

"Well, thank you. I'll bring it back tomorrow. Shall I help you clear up?" He motioned at the tray she brought out and the towel.

Brandy eyed the dishes and waved him off. "Oh, no! I got it. I have a dishwasher."

"Alright then. Goodnight, beautiful Brandy. I'll see you tomorrow."

Brandy's cheeks burned. "Goodnight, Rory."

She watched him walk away, waving when he turned at the fence, before taking the tea tray inside. She glanced out the window, but he was already gone from sight.

Brandy cleared up and locked the doors, sighing when she looked at the spot he'd been sitting.

Rory was like a dream – an incredibly handsome, charming dream. A man who had seemingly come from nowhere.

She'd lived here for six months and hadn't seen him once. The Shetland Islands weren't that big, and their tiny island of Unst had a population of less than a thousand. She thought she would have at least seen him around, particularly because he had a face someone wouldn't just look past.

Perhaps he was always working. He wanted to meet after the sun set, so maybe he worked all day and only had the evenings free. She tended to be home in the evening, preferring to do her shopping in the morning or afternoon, and she didn't go out for dinner because she didn't have any company.

That had to explain it.

Still, someone as attractive as him wouldn't go unnoticed by the other women around town. He could have his pick of women, so why was he single?

He worked long hours at sea. It was probably difficult for him to meet a good woman. Or he had some kind of issues he'd need to work past. Or . . . Brandy's heart sunk, maybe he just liked to play the field.

Still, she could find out. She could take it slow with him, find out what he was like, what kind of person he was. Even if he did play the field in the past, it didn't mean he wasn't interested in something serious with her.

Brandy went to bed happy, feeling as if everything was changing for the better as if a little bit of magic had found its way into her life.

~

The day seemed to drag while Brandy waited for four o'clock to roll around so she could start cooking. She wanted to impress him, so she started making pan-seared salmon, roasted parmesan potatoes, and broccoli. As she was cooking, she wished she'd have asked if he liked fish or had any allergies.

At 5:11, there was a knock on her door. She hurried to open it, smiling wide when she saw Rory, now dressed in jeans and a long-sleeved, navy-blue shirt, standing on her porch. She noticed he still wasn't wearing a coat.

"Hi."

"Hello."

She stepped back to let him in, her knees starting to shake when she realized how insanely hot he was, and he was in her house, about to have dinner with her.

"I should have asked yesterday, but you don't happen to have any allergies or aversions, do you?"

He shook his head as he stepped into the front room. "Nope."

Brandy sighed with relief. "Good. I'm making salmon. Is that alright?"

"That sounds delicious. Your home is beautiful, by the way."

"Thank you. I'm quite fond of it. Um … do you drink wine? I have a bottle I can bring out, or I can make some tea, or I have water."

"Wine sounds perfect. Is there anything I can do ta help in the kitchen?"

"Oh, no, thank you. It should be ready in just a few minutes."

She fetched the wine and a couple of glasses before heading back to the kitchen. As she was plating the food and setting it on the dining room table, Rory walked in, carrying two glasses and the bottle. He set them down beside their plates and took his seat.

"This looks amazing, Brandy."

"Thank you. Go ahead and help yourself." She sat across from him and took a sip of her wine.

"How was your day?" she asked after a few moments.

"It was good, actually. I told a friend about meeting you and having dinner with you. I've been excited."

"You did?" She couldn't hide her joy. "What did they say?"

Rory hesitated. "He told me to be careful."

"Careful?" She narrowed her eyes at him.

"He's afraid I'll get hurt."

"Oh." Her expression softened. So, he'd been burned before.

"Well, I promise not to hurt you."

"That's what I told him. Told him you were as kind as you are beautiful."

Brandy wanted to ask more, learn more about him and his past relationships, but she didn't want to press. He would tell her when he was ready.

"Oh, my god, this is incredible." Rory took another bite of salmon before pouring another glass of wine. "You're a fantastic cook, Brandy."

"Thank you."

"What do you do all day?" he asked.

"Oh, um. I'm a writer. So mostly, I daydream."

His eyes widened. "A writer, eh? That's pretty impressive. What do you write?"

"Fantasy with a bit of romance."

"Aye? That's great. I love both romance and fantasy. Do you have any books published?"

They talked for the next hour about Brandy's books. Rory took a particular interest in her story about a town being haunted by a kelpie.

"You got the town wrong. They live in Lock Coruisk."

Brandy laughed. "That may be so, but this is fiction."

Rory gently touched her cheek and leaned in, pressing his lips to hers. Her insides ignited at the tender touch.

He pulled away and looked into her eyes. "I hope I didn't overstep. You just look so beautiful."

Brandy bit back a smile. "You didn't overstep. That was perfect."

She leaned in and kissed him again. He made her feel warm, alive, wanted. It had been so long since she'd been with anyone, especially someone so sweet and sexy.

Panting heavily, Rory pulled Brandy onto his lap and stood. He walked, her legs wrapped around his waist, kissing her, to the couch, where he laid her down.

Brandy feverishly stripped off his shirt. She'd nearly forgotten how hot his body was. She ran her fingertips over his abs, trying to memorize this moment, this feeling. He pulled her shirt over her head and smiled at her before leaning down and kissing her again, hungrily.

So much for taking it slow.

~

Brandy awoke to Rory softly kissing her. She looked around her bedroom, dark because the sun still wasn't up.

“Hey.”

“I didn’t want to leave without telling you goodbye. I didn’t want you to wake up and see that I was gone and think that was all I wanted.”

“You’re leaving?”

“Sorry, beautiful. I have to be back to sea within the hour.”

Brandy nodded and sat up. “Alright.”

“Can I come back?” he asked. “Maybe tonight?”

Brandy grinned widely. “If you want.”

“I do. I really, really do.”

He kissed her again, and for a moment, she relived last night. The hours of kissing and touching and closeness were unlike anything she’d ever had before.

“Today is Thanksgiving in America. I was going to cook a big meal if you’re interested.”

Rory stroked her thigh, sending chills down her spine. “That sounds amazing. I’ll be here just after the sun goes down.” He kissed her again.

What she wouldn’t give to keep him there with her all day, lying in bed with her.

But before she could beg him to take the day off, he looked at the window, as the pale orange signaled the start of the day, and he hurried from the room.

~

Usually, Brandy would have started the turkey around nine in the morning, so dinner could be ready by two, but since Rory wasn’t going to be there until around five, and it was just the two of them, Brandy didn’t have to start the turkey until twelve. She enjoyed cooking for him, eager to discover what food he liked and what he didn’t.

She thought about him while she cooked, remembering the night before. The trail of kisses he’d left from her lips to her thigh. She missed him already.

It was impossible how much she liked him, after only knowing him for two days, but she did. She wanted him in her life more than she wanted anything else. She’d been unable to stop thinking about him since she first saw him.

Sure, he was sexy, but it was more than just physical attraction. It was like he clouded her brain, making it hard to think about anything but him. He was sweet and funny and seemed to like her.

She couldn't get over how he had woken her up to tell her bye. She'd never met a guy like that before. Most of the men in her past wouldn't have bothered. They'd just call when they were ready for another booty call.

Brandy wondered if she had jumped into bed with him too quickly. She should have waited a few months, weeks at least, but there was something about Rory that screamed out to her to kiss him, to give him everything, all of her.

And she'd gladly do it.

Brandy shook her thoughts away as she set the table. Remembering how he had liked the wine, she'd bought a few more bottles and left them to chill.

As promised, Rory arrived just after the sun set. He looked handsome, even just casually dressed in jeans and a tee-shirt. Brandy filled two glasses of wine and brought him one.

Rory accepted the glass with a smile. "Dinner smells amazing."

"I just finished. You ready to eat?"

"Absolutely. I'm starving."

They chatted through dinner. Rory told her about a guy named Mack that he worked with who caught a fish and insisted on giving it to the new recruit, Samuel. He spoke as if he thought highly of him. Brandy couldn't help but smile. Learning more about Rory and what he did all day made her like him all the more.

"It was a fantastic day. Mack's the one I told about you. He asked why I didn't come home last night, and I told him I was with you."

"You live with Mack?" Brandy was surprised. They hadn't covered where he lived the night before.

"Well, yeah, but that's just how it is. He's just a friend," he added as if assuming Brandy would think something more.

Brandy laughed. "Good. No, I'm glad you have someone. Mack sounds like a good guy."

"Oh, he is. Maybe you can meet him one day."

"I would love to."

Rory spent the night again. Brandy slept, wrapped in his arms, breathing in his scent, trying to remember every last detail about him. She was so afraid to lose him – so afraid of being alone again.

Morning came, and Brandy woke up to a breakfast of eggs, toast, and coffee. Rory had woken up early to make them breakfast in bed.

He hurried off again, promising to come back that night. Brandy sat in the bed, staring at the door he disappeared through, and hugged her knees, wishing it was already time for dinner so she could see him again.

She couldn't deny it. She was falling in love with Rory.

~

"How can you love a guy you've known for three days?" Sarah asked over video chat.

Brandy shrugged. "It feels like more than that, to be honest. He's just so sweet and charming, and he seems to care about my feelings."

Sarah smacked her lips. Tabitha, Sarah's three-year-old daughter, screamed in the background. "All men start off like that. Then before you know it, you have two kids and he's never home."

"He isn't like that."

"Oh, come on!"

"I'm serious."

"Well, I'm coming out for New Years. I'll meet him then and be the judge."

Brandy laughed. "Alright, deal."

Tabitha screamed again, and this time Timothy, Sarah's one-year-old, started crying. "Oh, God. I have to go. The kids are being monsters."

"Tell them Auntie Brandy loves them!"

Brandy hung up and set her phone down. She looked out the window, toward the ocean, and saw something swimming. She wrapped her cardigan around her and stepped out into the blistering cold. The wind whipped her hair around her face as she walked to the edge of the property to get a better look.

Not too far off, there swam a small raft of seals. Brandy smiled as she watched them play. After a few moments, she wrapped her cardigan tighter around her and made her way inside to make some hot chocolate. If she didn't sit down and get some work done and sent to her publisher, she'd be in trouble.

She sat at her computer and started writing. She wrote for hours about a woman who fell in love with a fairy.

Maybe she was projecting some of her own feelings onto her character, but she wrote the fairy with a lot of Rory's traits.

She looked out the window and smiled when she saw him walking up the sidewalk. She hurried to the door and opened it as soon as he stepped onto the porch.

"Hi," she breathed, wrapping her arms around him.

"Hello, beautiful. How was your day?"

"Better now that you're back."

~

Before Brandy knew it, Christmas was there. Rory had come by every night, and Brandy had almost forgotten what it was like to sleep without him. He was warm and felt safe.

Christmas morning arrived, and Rory woke Brandy up with a kiss and a platter of chocolate chip pancakes, her favorite.

"Don't tell me you're leaving!" she cried, grabbing his hand.

"I have ta. I'm sorry, love. I would stay with you all day if I could."

"But it's Christmas!"

"I know." He kissed her forehead and wrapped his arms around her. "That's why I hate that I have ta go so badly. But …" he pulled away and reached across her to the bedside table. There was a small present, carefully wrapped in gold paper. "I got you a present."

Brandy ripped off the paper and found a small, square box, about the size of her palm. She opened it and gasped at the pearl necklace. It was beautiful. She only hoped it hadn't cost him a fortune.

"They're gorgeous!" she said, looking from him to the necklace. "But … please tell me they aren't real."

"They are. Is that a problem?"

Nobody had ever got her such an extravagant gift before. "It's just such an expensive present."

"It's a family heirloom. It belonged to my mother."

Tears stung her eyes. She threw her arms around Rory and hugged him. He was the sweetest, most thoughtful man she'd ever known.

"I love you, Rory," she whispered.

He returned the hug, kissed her head. "I love you too, Brandy."

~

Rory was gone before the sun came up, but he was back as soon as the sun went down. Brandy had made another feast and put on her sexiest black dress and heels. She handed him his gift, which was nowhere near as perfect as what he gave her, and they enjoyed an evening by the fire, sipping wine.

Brandy sat on the couch, snuggled up next to Rory, and told him stories about Christmas' when she was little. Her dad always went overboard with gifts and snacks. He made just about every cookie imaginable, and they'd go around the neighborhood, handing them out. Once she was older, Brandy realized he was trying to make up for the fact that her mother wasn't there.

"My favorite Christmas was four years ago when Sarah announced she was pregnant. I never saw Dad so happy. He wanted to be a grandpa more than anything. See, she and Max had just gotten married, and Dad told her at the wedding he wanted a few grandkids. So, when she told him, he brought out the eggnog to celebrate, non-alcoholic for Sarah, of course."

Brandy smiled at the memory.

"Sounds wonderful."

"It was. She got pregnant with Timothy right after Dad died. We took it as a sign that he was still with us, in a way, and she named him after him."

Brandy thought for a moment on the memory, then gasped. "Oh, my God."

"What's the matter? Did I do something?"

"No, I …"

How could she be so foolish? So reckless?

She was late.

She'd stopped taking birth control when she moved, but she still took her daily vitamins, she had somehow managed to forget.

And she was so head over heels for Rory she didn't stop and ask about a condom.

She put on a smile, determined not to say anything until she knew for certain. She made a mental note to pick up a pregnancy test in the morning.

Rory didn't fall for it. "What's going on?"

"Well … I was just remembering Sarah announcing she was pregnant on Christmas, and it made me realize I haven't had a period since before I met you."

"Oh." Rory stared at her for a moment. "Oh!" A wide grin spread across his face. "Really? You might be …"

Brandy swallowed. "Yeah. I might be pregnant."

Rory laughed. "Well, you can have the scarf back. This might be the best gift I could get."

"You aren't upset?"

"Why on earth would I be upset? It's a baby! You could be pregnant with our baby! Brandy, my love, that's the most magical gift you could ever give me."

Tears filled her eyes. "But we just met. We aren't even married."

"Technicalities. I love you, and you love me. And if you have a baby, I'm going to love it. No matter what."

Brandy sniffled and kissed him. She had no idea how she'd managed to get so lucky.

~

"Oh, my goodness! Your house is amazing, but damn if this isn't the coldest place on earth."

Brandy laughed at her sister and poured the freshly brewed coffee. The kids were in the living room, playing with the toys Brandy had bought them while Christmas music played softly in the background.

"You adjust after a while."

"I don't see how. Not after growing up in sunny Florida."

"I'm sorry Max couldn't make it," Brandy said, pouring herself a cup of coffee.

"Me too. He couldn't leave his mom in the state she's in though."

"Her dementia that bad?"

Sarah nodded. "Yeah. Poor thing doesn't have long."

They sat at the kitchen table. Sarah sat facing the living room to keep her eye on the kids. Brandy wondered if she'd be that protective, where she'd need to watch her baby at all times to make sure they were alright.

Sarah was a good mother. Brandy hoped she could be like her, but she wasn't entirely sure. Kids were hard work. Sometimes she would listen to her niece and nephew screaming and crying and wonder why people would have more than one.

"Where's your man?" Sarah asked.

"Working. From sun up to sundown. Every. Single. Day."

Sarah narrowed her eyes. "That's weird. What's he do?"

"He's a fisherman. Works with a guy named Mack, who he looks up to. I think Mack kind of took over as a father figure since Rory's parents died."

"Well, that's sweet."

"It is. Rory is sweet. Really, he's amazing. You're going to love him. Just wait until dinner."

Brandy wasn't wrong. It wasn't but thirty minutes into dinner when Sarah mouthed, "I love him!" so only Brandy could see. What wasn't there to love? Rory was nearly perfect, and he showed how much he cared about Brandy.

"Did you tell her yet?" he asked during dessert.

Brandy shot him a look, then looked down at her slice of cake.

"No, I didn't, but now I suppose I should."

"Tell me what?"

"I'm sorry, love. If you want to wait, I can lie," he whispered, leaning in close.

His breath on her neck gave her chill bumps, and she smiled.

"No. It's alright. I was going to tell her before she left anyway."

"Tell me what?" Sarah repeated, feeding Timothy a tiny bite of cake.

"Tell you that Rory and I are going to have a baby."

Sarah dropped the spoon and stared at Brandy, mouth agape. Timothy grunted and tried to reach the cake. "Um … how? You just met!"

"Happy accident?"

"I prefer surprise," Rory chimed.

Sarah glared at him. "Accident is more accurate."

"Sarah!"

"Look, I know it isn't any of my business, but I'm worried about you, Brandy. A baby will change your life upside down. I love my kids, I do," she picked up the spoon and gave whimpering Anthony another bite, "but sometimes they drive me absolutely crazy. And I just thought you'd get to live a little before you settled down and started a family."

"I am living, sweetie. Look at me! I'm in Scotland. I'm with this extremely sexy, sweet man, who loves me and wants to step up and be a dad. I'm so lucky. Sure, I'm scared, but I need you on my side. We're happy."

"What if it doesn't work out?" She looked from Brandy to Rory.

"I'm not going anywhere," Rory told her. "I'm here for her as long as she wants me."

"But you won't be here. From morning to evening, you're not here. It will all fall to her."

"Then from evening to morning, I'll take care of the baby while Brandy rests."

A warmth of appreciation spread through Brandy. Rory was amazing. She really was lucky.

Sarah sighed, then looked at her sister. "Alright," she said. "Okay. If you're happy, then I'll be happy for you."

"Thank you."

~

The months flew by as they stayed in their bubble of happiness. Rory stayed at sea all day, then after dinner, he'd work on getting things ready for the baby. He painted the nursery a light blue and decorated it with clouds and rainbows. He put together the crib and nursery furniture while Brandy sorted through the clothes they had bought for their beautiful baby boy.

Finally, the due date came. Brandy begged Rory to stay home, but, with tears in his eyes, he insisted he didn't have a choice.

Although she said she understood, she didn't. She cried as soon as he left. He'd missed every appointment, every ultrasound because he had work, but today was supposed to be different. He was supposed to be with her this week, prepared at a moment's notice to get her to the hospital to have their baby.

It was his job – his one job during labor – to make sure she was comfortable. How was she supposed to be comfortable when she very well might be doing it alone?

Brandy double-checked her go-bag had everything she needed, ready to go. She walked around the house all day, but nothing happened.

Rory came home, excited he hadn't missed the birth, but soon, it was time for him to leave again.

Brandy couldn't control her tears anymore. She needed him with her.

"Please, don't go!" she begged. "I can't do this alone!"

Rory swallowed and hugged her, avoiding her round belly. "I'm so sorry, my love. Please forgive me."

And he left.

Brandy cried until it stopped hurting, but a sharp pain in her belly told her it was about to hurt a lot worse.

She called a taxi and wrote a note for Rory, telling him she was at the hospital. She called Sarah while she waited.

"Did you at least have breakfast yet?"

"No. You aren't supposed to eat when you're in labor."

"Yeah, but you're going to be there for hours and hours. Trust me, you're going to regret not eating."

"I gotta go. I'll call you later."

"Good luck, honey! Love you!"

Sarah had been right. The day passed, and labor was slow. Painful and slow. As she paced around the small hospital room, she wished she would have had breakfast. With every contraction, she cursed Rory for not being with her – for not being as scared and miserable as she was.

Evening came, and Rory rushed into the hospital room. "Am I too late?"

Brandy laid back in the bed and cried. She didn't care how mad she'd been with him all day for leaving her to do this alone. He was there, and that was all that mattered. He rubbed her swollen belly and kissed her head.

"I'm here, beautiful. I'm so sorry I wasn't here. How much longer do you got?"

"I was dilated eight. The doctors are about to check again, though."

It was showtime. After several long minutes of pushing, Robert was born. His cry filled the room, and for a moment, nothing but that beautiful sound mattered to Brandy. He was here, he was fine.

They laid him in her arms and the flood of joy and relief overwhelmed her. He was so beautiful, so perfect, just like his daddy.

~

Robert was a sweet baby for a couple of months, then colic set in, and he didn't want to sleep anymore. He was up almost all day and all night. As promised, Rory took over when he got home, but Brandy missed him. They almost never had a spare moment together anymore.

He was kissing her goodbye one morning when Robert was nearly three months old. It was their one-year anniversary. One year since they first met – first started seeing one another.

"Can't you please just stay? For me? For today?"

"I can't, love. You know that."

The anger had been building for a while, but usually, she could control her emotions. Not today though.

"Why? Why can't you just have one day off work? What's so important about this job that you have to work seven days a week?"

"It isn't a job, love, it's my life. It's who I am!"

Brandy shook her head. "That's bullshit."

He looked hurt. "Brandy … when have I ever lied to you?"

She shook her head and crossed her arms in front of her chest.

"You could stay home for once."

He stood and backed away, running his fingers through his hair.

"I can't. I have to be back at sea before the sun comes up or I can never return. It isn't an option for me, Brandy. It's my home!"

She was on her feet before she could stop herself.

"This should be your home! Here with me and Robert! If they fire you, they fire you! We can find you another job!"

He shook his head. "Yer not listening. It isn't a job, my love." He looked into her eyes and swallowed. "Mack said not to tell you, but you have to know. You deserve to know. I never wanted to hide this part of who I am from you, but I was scared. Foolish and scared and madly in love." He took her hands in his.

Her heart and mind raced. What was it? What was he hiding?

"I'm a selkie."

Brandy shook her head. "The seal people? That's ridiculous. Selkies aren't real."

Rory looked out the window at the rising sun, looking hopeless. "We are real. Very much so. And if I don't go now, I'll never be able to go back. My skin will dry out in the sun, and I'll never get it back on proper."

"Don't act like I'm stupid, Rory! I'm not a child who's going to believe some fantasy."

"I'm not lying to you."

She crossed her arms, sighing heavily. "Okay. Answer me this. If you aren't working, how do you seem to always have money?"

"My colony has a deal with some of the local fishermen. We find the fish and they'll pay us for our work. We can make twice as much as them, twice as fast." He looked out the window again. The sky was turning orange, signaling the start of the day. "I have to go. I'll be back tonight, and we can talk then."

"Oh, my God." She threw her hands up as tears stung her eyes.

"Forget it. Just go, Rory. Go. Get out of my house."

"Brandy …" He reached for her hands again, but she pulled away.

"No. I wouldn't want to keep you from the sea and your seal skin." Her lip curled up. "Just get out." Her voice broke. She'd never felt more betrayed. "Don't bother with coming back. I wouldn't want to burden you with human life."

"Brandy …"

"Go, Rory!"

She glared at him so hard he backed away. She turned away and he ran from the room. She looked out the window and saw him running across the backyard, toward the hill where she had seen him for the first time a year ago.

Robert started to cry.

After taking a deep breath, Brandy wiped her eyes and went to get Robert a bottle.

~

Rory didn't come home. Brandy stood by the back door, looking out over the hill, waiting for him to come back. The sun sank lower and lower until it disappeared, but still, Rory didn't come.

She'd got what she asked for, but it didn't make her feel better.

He had lied right to her face, and all because she'd asked him to stay home with her.

She just wanted one day. Just one day to be with him, to celebrate their anniversary.

Why would he think she would believe such a far-fetched excuse? Because she was a fantasy writer? Because she loved the idea of humans and mythological creatures falling in love?

She wiped her eyes and turned away from the back door. It was time to get Robert to bed.

He was exceptionally calm tonight. Perhaps he knew his parents had fought and Brandy needed some quiet time to think. Maybe he knew how sad she was, and he wanted to be calm, for her.

Whatever the reason, Brandy was grateful when she laid him down in his crib, and he didn't wake up.

She brushed his hair off his forehead and tears filled her eyes. He looked so much like his daddy. He was so handsome already, and the years were only going to make him better.

She went back to the kitchen to stare out the door. Rory should have been home by now, but he wasn't coming. She'd blew up and scared him off.

She had expected him to come back, though. To talk to her, tell her what he meant because surely, he had meant something different than what he said.

He wasn't a liar, and he never talked down to her, so what was all that about being a selkie?

Brandy thought about the seals she had seen right after she had just met him. She had seen them a few times throughout the past year, but always during the day. But that's how seals lived, wasn't it? They went back to the sea during the night.

What if …?

Brandy shook her head and locked the door.

No. She was being stupid. There was no such thing as selkies.

~

Rory didn't come back. It had been a week, and he still hadn't tried to contact Brandy. She had thought he might at least want to come to see Robert, even if he didn't want anything to do with Brandy.

After putting Robert to bed, Brandy made herself a cup of tea, wrapped a blanket around herself, made sure the baby monitor was still hooked to her pants and walked to the edge of the property. She sat in the swing and stared out at the sea.

His life was the sea. He had told her that. Wasn't that true of all fishermen? They loved their families, but their life belonged to the sea.

She hugged her knees and cried, wishing more than anything Rory would come home and tell her he still loved her.

That's when she saw it. It was difficult to see in the darkness, but the moonlight showed a lone, brown seal swimming for the shore. Brandy narrowed her eyes as she watched it come ashore. It flipped its head back a few times, lifting its flippers toward its face.

Brandy gasped when she saw a human man pull down the sealskin and step out into the night, stark naked.

Brandy dropped her tea and ran, dropping the blanket, down the hill, toward the beach. Rory was back.

He hadn't been lying. It had been a far-fetched fantasy, but it was a true fantasy, one she was living.

She made it to the beach to see he was fully dressed, wearing the scarf she had given him for Christmas last year. She ran, as fast as the sand would allow, and jumped into his arms.

His kiss was warmer than she remembered, and she never wanted him to stop. She never wanted to let him go again because if she did, she might lose him forever.

But he pulled away and she started to cry. "I'm so sorry I didn't believe you."

"I'm sorry I waited so long to tell ya. Can you forgive me?"

Brandy nodded and kissed him again. "Are you coming home?"

"As long as you want me."

"I always want you. I was just mad. I didn't understand. I do now."

They walked home, hand in hand, and Rory kissed sleeping Robert on his head. After making sure he was still sound asleep, he turned back to Brandy.

"I need you to understand that I have to go back. Every day. No matter what."

Brandy nodded. "Okay. I can make plans for after the sun goes down. We can make it work."

Rory smiled, sending shivers through Brandy. He was so much sexier when he smiled.

"You're okay with me, then? My being away? My being a selkie?"

Brandy nodded. "So long as you always come home to me."

He kissed her, soft and quick. "I count down the minutes when I'm away until I can see you again, Brandy."

He meant it; she knew he did. "I love you so much, Rory."

He kissed her, licking her lips, tasting her tongue, and she was afire with desire. She'd missed him so much – too much.

He lifted her up, and she wrapped her legs around his hips. He carried her to their bedroom, where he laid her down and stripped off his shirt.

"Wait!" he said, suddenly, pulling away from her.

Brandy sat up, breathless, already lost in passion and longing. "What?"

"I brought you this. It was going to be your Christmas present, but I don't want to wait anymore."

He pulled out a small box and opened it, revealing a diamond ring.

"Brandy, my beautiful angel, will you marry me?"

Brandy smiled, tears filling her eyes. "Promise you'll come home every night?"

Rory laughed and nodded. "Yes, my love. I will come home to you every single night."

"Then yes!" She put the ring on her finger and kissed him.

"I love you, Brandy," he whispered, laying her down and pressing against her.

She had never been happier to be proven wrong. Rory was back, and he was hers forever.

Every night, she and Robert would watch the sun go down and wait, watching the sea for Rory to come home.

Robert grew big enough to jump and waved when he saw his daddy swimming to shore. Rory waved back and excitement filled Brandy.

She touched her stomach and smiled.

Rory picked Robert up and hugged him and Brandy.

She took his hand and kissed him, before telling him Robert was going to be a big brother. Rory yelled with excitement and spun her and Robert around.

As she watched her husband rock their son to sleep, Brandy sighed. This was all she wanted when she moved here – to find a family and a life of her own that she could be proud of.

Rory smiled at Brandy, making her heart flutter. She hadn't been lonely in three years, and she'd never be alone again.

Freshies and Sea Folk

Sara Mosier

Clarity stretched his golden-brown tail across the gritty shore, pulling away the cotton-wood sprouts at the small of his back and tossing them aside. He'd fallen asleep in the sun again, this lake was relatively quiet, not a lot of humans and the ones that did show up were usually boating and drunk. He could slink around the murky water and mimic a crocodile, for safety or simply just for shits and giggles.

The lake was met up with a river so every now and again he'd have a visit from a sea creature, far and few in between but amusing, nonetheless. They were particularly easy to scare which Clarity always found equally amusing given there were far scarier creatures in the ocean. Not that he'd moved out that far, too dangerous, and the salt water dried out his skin. As if the sun wasn't harsh enough on his cheeks and shoulders.

He could hear a boat nearby, the human music blaring, it reverberated through the water in a muffled way that was soothing. He sank down into the muddy water, raising his arms high above his head to fall faster, taking a deep breath of the earthy taste of his home. As his bottom hit the floor of the lake, he was startled by a large whooshing past him, twirling him physically in a circle, pulling up the silt from the lake floor and clouding everything around him.

He broke the surface, spitting the sand out of his mouth, "What the hell?!" His eyes scanned the water around him, trying to see if it were simply a large fish, but it wasn't, the lake was quiet. He knew for sure that it must have been something that wandered in from the ocean, it did rain heavily the night before. He'd found a few things that had blown into the water that he would add to his collection in his cove. It wasn't completely out of the question that this something was a person.

"Who are you?" A question broke the ear-shattering silence.

Clarity spun around, up near a cluster of rocks was a pale face, turquoise eyes and probably the brightest tail Clarity had ever seen in his short lifetime. It, or he, Clarity wasn't exactly sure, was hiding their tail curled close to their body, long hair looking like silvery moss. He wasn't even sure if he'd seen this color before. It looked like the shiny rocks he searched for in underwater caves. Well, suffice it to say, they were beautiful.

"Howdy," he grinned, swimming slowly but closer, "Haven't seen you around these parts…"

"I don't know where I am." They replied petulantly, but it was to hide fear, it was far too obvious and echoed off the walls of Clarity's nearby cove.

"Well, you don't look like you're from around here. That's some nice hair or is that moss? Oh, hey you're from the ocean aren't you!"

They flinched, significantly so with the splashing of water, "I suppose. I-I came down this strip of water and I became trapped in some kind of...netting...." They raised their tail with a frown.

"Goddamn fishermen…" Clarity growled, "Well, come'ere." But the other merperson flinched once more and fell backwards into the water, pulling their long hair up and over their eyes. They began shrieking in fear so Clarity dove into the water to get to their side faster. "Hold your horses! Geez!" He put out one hand and nudged away the silvery hair, then retracted.

The stranger lurched back even more dramatically and promptly knocked themselves out, Clarity knew so because the other went completely limp in his arms. There was an alarming blooming of red in the water left in its wake.

He kept them both upright in the water, looked around once more, and swam towards his cove. He swam on his back keeping both their heads just above the surface and moved as fast as he could, "And to think today was a quiet one."

It took more time than he cared to admit but he dragged the heavy but lithe body of the stranger into his home, pulled him up at the edge of the moss-covered shore, and took a much-needed breath, "Fuck, for a skinny ass you sure are heavy…"

He had a thought, did seamaids . . . or ermm . . . seamerpeople…. whatever, need to be underwater?

He could do both, but he honestly didn't know too much about the ocean folk. He situated them up on the soft make-shift bed he used for sleeping and went to work on the netting. He could see it had considerably cut into their flesh and as soon as he touched their tail, he heard a loud whimper that made him pause.

"Hey, hey, you're alright, gonna get this off." he said more to himself as the other's eyes weren't open. He used a knife he'd found at the bottom of a fishing boat several years ago and cut through the netting. The way that it had cut into their flesh he wondered just how long it had been there. Because as he pulled it away it began to bleed, brilliantly red, and it fell in droplets into the water. It really was a good thing that Clarity came upon them and not a predator. Because this particular creature was lean, trim, and smaller, quite the easy catch.

The rest of the net fell away, Clarity pushed them farther up onto the shore, curling their long, brightly colored tail up and out of the water. He made a makeshift bandage out of dry grass, then went about checking their head for any wounds. Besides the small gash on the back of their head, there was nothing that seemed to be life-threatening. Or at least hoped this was unfortunately his first time meeting a speaking person from the sea.

Those shockingly blue eyes rolled open, finally, "Hey, there ya are." But this time he kept hold of both their arms, "Hey, hey, hey, none of that...I just got you fixed up."

"Where am I?"

"Well, this is kind of my home." he looked around, "Not much but I think it's cozy. Good place to stay out of the storms and stuff. Like the one you got caught up in. Hey, you got a name?"

They swallowed visibly hard, bringing one hand to the bump on their head, and then studied their long pale fingers. "C-Calliope…"

"Calliope...that's a really pretty name, don't think I've heard of it...where'd you learn to speak human?"

"S-Ships...near islands...what my father has taught me…"

"You don't have to be afraid of me, sweetheart, I got no reason to hurt you. Besides, why would I have bandaged you up?" He swam over and shimmied his way onto the shore to sit.

This made the creature, now known as Calliope, examine their tail, "O-oh thank you I hadn't noticed...this...this hurts…"

“Haven’t you ever hurt yourself? Ocean is a lot bigger than this joint…”

“I don’t leave my home often…it’s forbidden…is the best word for it I suppose.” they replied shyly and now Clarity could see how exhausted they were, “I’m afraid I might not know the way home. There was a big storm….and I should have gone back a-and the waves caught me up…”

“Hey, hey, hey, no need to get upset, not like you’re alone I’ll help you out I promise.”

Calliope grimaced, “Why help me?”

“Have you done something evil I don’t know about? Like I don't know, sink a ship?”

Calliope’s eyes went wide, and that delicate-looking hand went to their chest. “Heavens no!”

Clarity began to laugh, “Oh you are fun.”

Calliope crossed their arms and growled.

“See,” Clarity said pointing, “That just makes you cuter, now how’s about getting some shut-eye and I’ll get us some grub.”

“I am not cute, and I do not like being made fun of nor am I hungry or tired….”

“Says the three-year-old... okay my friend, you do your thing, but I’d suggest sticking around here until you can move better cause this might not be the ocean, but we got Croc’s that’ll rip that pretty face off. Also, this is storm season, one could crop up out of nowhere and you’d be in mighty big trouble.”

When Calliope’s eyes went genuinely wide Clarity frowned, “Oh don’t worry I just don’t want you gettin’ into trouble. I’ll find you your way back no worries. Just ya know rest, relax do whatever you do when you’re not swimming around being royalty.”

“Royalty?”

This particular mer was adorable and Clarity hadn’t been this amused or excited about another living being in front of him in quite some time. The drunken boaters didn’t count and really, there weren’t a lot of other merfolk around here. Unlike the ocean folk, lake folk stayed by themselves. His parents made him and split. Which was a little out of the norm, but he managed all on his own and maybe he learned a little too much from the humans but hey, at least things were interesting, today proved that.

“Nevermind, man, you take everything literally don’t ya. Stay here,” he put out hands, and waved downwards, “Stay, and I’ll be right back.”

“O-Okay,” Calliope gulped, “I-I’ll stay here I am feeling a bit woozy.”

Clarity nodded, “See? I knew it. Okay, I’ll be back in a flash.”

~

Clarity knew he needed to hurry, for all he knew this little ocean dude or dudette would flitter off, and despite being amused he didn’t think he would be able to sleep at night if he thought they weren’t safe or worse getting eaten by the number of possibilities out there. As he swam along the outskirt shores of his cove, heading for a thick seaweed bed, he passed a friend of his, “Clarity hey,” she smiled, only coming out of the water enough to show her head, “The rain really did us good, look at this loot!” she held up a handful of the seaweed. “It’s really good, here I’ll share, man you’ve gotten a lot of sun . . .”

“Thanks, Leddy, and yeah fell asleep a few times on the shore. It’s hot!” he swam to her and took the food from her hands, “I found someone from that storm.”

She delicately put the plant between her teeth and chewed, “What, like a person? A human? I’m not surprised those idiots don’t seem to understand that boating when the winds are so high isn’t a good idea. Not to mention they’re usually drunk.”

“No not a human, another merperson, a salty, not a freshie! I’ve never seen one, isn’t that wild?

“Whoooa, that is wild my dad saw one, one time, but uh it wasn’t exactly alive. So, I haven’t seen one either.”

“Well, this one is alive, pretty and hurt, I gotta get them some food. Maybe some shrimp, have you seen any around here lately? Everything’s pretty quiet after that kind of rain.”

“Hmm, southeast cove, sometimes the wind pushes them towards the shore. So, am I gonna get to meet this salty?”

He couldn’t help but make a face. “They seem kinda shy, and tired too. I don't know how long they were caught up in one of those goddamn fishing traps, but it was at least most of today.”

“Well, if you need help hunting let me know.” she shrugged, her hair was the color of the lake water, green and tawny, so when she dipped, he had to focus. She flitted her tail, dove into the muddy waters, and disappeared.

He followed Leddy’s instructions and was able to find quite a bit of shrimp, and more dry grass to make a bed on the mantle of his cave.

He nearly dropped the collection of his hunting trip when he re-entered his home, he shoved everything up onto the nearest ledge and swam fast over to his charge when he found them unmoving, “Hey, you doing okay?”

“I-I am more tired than I first thought....” he was slumped almost completely into the water and shivering.

“Let’s get you up into the grass bed and I’ll make a fire.”

“A what?” they slurred.

“Human stuff I learned; it creates heat…”

“Like…” Calliope ran their tongue over their lips, “Like the heat vents...near the...the volcanos…”

“Uh, sure, just like that,” He pulled the other merperson up onto the bed of seaweed and grass, “Lay down, little higher, there ya go…” He ended up pulling Calliope bodily until they were completely out of the water.

“Thank you…” they whispered, snuggling into the soft bed provided, “This is warm too…”

“Good, that’s good,” he went to work building the fire and soon enough had it filling heat into the tiny cave. He laid back on his own grass bed that Leddy had provided. There were always the best wet grass sheddings after a storm. The warmth filled the concave space, Clarity was lulled by the silence, the gentle beating of the waves against the cave walls, and the sleepy breathing of his new guest.

Just as his eyes were closing, he thought he could get used to this. He wasn’t usually very social, and no one had ever stayed in his home other than Leddy. It wasn’t that he thought that he was particularly unlikeable; he'd just learned to live alone ever since he was little. He’d resigned himself to the fact that he just was meant to be alone. But as his eyes strayed across the expanse of the cave, Calliope with their skin so fair it could shine and beautiful scales, a cute impish like smile on their mouths as they slept in comfort, he realized how empty things had seemed.

It was late in the evening when Clarity woke from his nap, the reason being the whimpering sound that finally broke through his deep sleep. He sat up, confused for a few moments before he realized Calliope had nearly slid back into the water, the fire had dampened, and he figured they must have gotten cold.

He shimmied over the surface of the cave shelf and placed a hand on the top of their very silvery hair, it was so soft there weren't proper words. Like the cottony l moss that grew on rocks close to the shores. He found it endearing, and he wasn't sure why the other was so lithe and easy to move. . . He carefully and slowly took them underneath the arms and pulled them up onto the dry grass once more. The grass he'd weaved together he covered over him like a blanket he'd seen humans use when they were sleeping at the head of their boats in the sun. They usually were laying on those multicolored blankets but sometimes the sun proved to be too much, and they'd pull them over their pink skin. Skin that looked similar to his friend here, it was so fair, and he had to wonder how many times Calliope surfaced. He also began to wonder what made him want to explore past his ocean home.

Just as the thought crossed his mind they began to stir, their pale brows wrinkling in distress. He opened his mouth to speak but Calliope wrenched out of sleep perfectly nailing his forehead against Clarity. Both screeched and fell backwards. Calliope cried out louder and shriller.

"Goddamn dude, calm down…oh shit…" he cried holding his head, it felt as though someone had slammed him with a rock.

"That was not my intention I assure you." Calliope groaned, their eyes pinched shut, and pitched forward against the grass.

"I think you were having a bad dream or something. I thought you'd gotten cold, and I think I was right…fuck…are you okay?" Clarity tried to dampen his tone and not sound so cross, but it was hard to do with how badly his head was throbbing, he checked his fingers for blood and then suddenly worried Calliope might have a wound.

"I believe so…" they said, muffled into the palms of their hands, "I am so sorry…"

“That’s okay…no damage done…I don’t think so anyway. You aren’t bleeding again, are you?”

They checked their fingertips, blinking firmly still, “No, I don’t believe so. That…has never happened before.”

“What, a bad dream?” Clarity asked, moving forward to put more dry wood in the dying flame that was dancing colors of orange and gold off Calliope’s flesh.

“A bad dream…no…I haven’t…I was being chased. By men. They had those nets that cut me…that caught me…”

Clarity stopped stoking the fire, a tendril of fear passing across his skin, “Was someone chasing you before you got here? Is that how you got caught up or was it just the storm.”

They were still cradling their head but had sat up enough to be sitting straight, “I-I’m afraid I’m having trouble remembering. I hit my head rather hard. Everything was so chaotic; the storm came in so fast…it was dark…I heard…I heard an engine and then my head hit something. It left me a bit dizzy and the last thing I remember was being dragged. I woke up in that cove you found me in and I’m not exactly sure how I got there.”

“I didn’t see any boats nearby…at least I didn’t think so. I think it would be a good idea if you stuck around here for a while. If they were fishermen and they knew what they were seeing that could mean trouble.”

Their eyes went wide and glassy and far too close to tears for Clarity’s taste, “If there were men, will they come back? Will they find me here? I’ve never been so close to humans I know not what to do to avoid them! I was so stupid how could I have been so stupid! I could have died, my father warned me, he said they eat us, capture us, use us…”

Clarity took it upon himself to move into the other’s space and put his arms around him, scooping him close to his chest and cradling one hand to the back of his head, carefully to avoid the bump, “You’re safe here, nothin’ is gonna get ya I won’t let it.”

Calliope went completely stock still, “W-What are you doing?”

Clarity had to laugh, “I’m hugging you, ya big, adorable idiot. It’s what the land folk do.” he joked, but then it wasn’t completely because he’d never hugged anyone besides his closest friends. He didn’t know what it was like to have a family or parents, but Calliope seemed to be in the same boat despite speaking of having one. “Is that okay? Is this okay?” he thought to ask.

“Y-Yes, it’s nice…this hugging…” And he felt them relax, slumping just in the slightest and huffing a breath when they rested their face in the crook of his neck.

“You’ve never been hugged?” He thought it was best to keep his mind off fishermen and their nets and spears. “You said you had a dad…”

Calliope cut him off sharply, tightening his hold even though his voice sounded like he might run, “Father doesn’t touch…or hug…or even value his children. I am simply a tool to bring two kingdoms together.”

“Is that why you ran away?” when Calliope gave a small shrug Clarity refrained from rolling his eyes, continuing to pat their back, “I mean swam away I guess you can’t run can you. . .same concept though.”

“I don’t wanna go back…” they spoke barely above a whisper, “Please don’t make me go back.”

Now it was Clarity’s turn to go still, frozen, and afraid. He continued the gentle touches, given that he wasn’t told to stop, and began to rock the smaller merperson, “You don’t have to. I-I mean we’ll figure something out. Besides. . .” He pulled away, so they were face to face, their face was pale but flushed, to the point that it looked like they’d splashed their cheeks with paint. “You’re safe here. I promise those men or your dad, whatever, can’t find you here. I’ve lived here a long time, at least twelve years and you're the first sea person I’ve come across. Leddy is the only one that knows about my home.”

“Truly?”

Their language was so proper it reminded him of the yacht people that stayed at the port, those people annoyed him but not Calliope, despite the scary situation of having a new roommate on the run he found it adorable. “Yes, truly, you can stay here as long as you want. I mean, it’s a big enough place, it is a cave after all.”

Now Calliope was certainly snuggling, “I’m warm now, but can we stay like this until I go back to sleep? T-then you can leave to your side if you’d wish.”

“If you had any idea what a puppy was, that's what I’d call you. A slightly larger puppy.” He was already situating them both more comfortably, he made a full blanket out of the grass he’d gathered earlier up and around them, the fire was blazing now making it look like the early morning hours when it was still in the dead of night. He could smell it on the riverbank, he could see through the small holes in the ceiling that the moon was still rising high in the sky.

This. This he had never had, this was a level of intimacy he wasn’t sure existed, Calliope happily burrowed in against his chest, wiggling with emphasis, and taking haven beneath the grass blanket. When they exhaled loudly and contently Clarity smiled. “You’ll feel better tomorrow. Sleep always makes things better in my opinion.”

Calliope pressed their forehead over his heart, “Thank you…”

“Sure, not a problem.” What he didn’t say was how thankful he’d come upon the smaller merperson. He didn’t wanna think about a croc getting him, a bigger fish or any number of strange creatures that lived on the bottom of the lake, things that had drifted in from the ocean that not even Clarity was aware of. He held them a little tighter, running fingers up and down their purplish, pale skin, taking note of the goosebumps and how now their body was much warmer than it had been a few minutes before.

Before he could stop himself, he kissed the crown of their head and fell asleep as well.

~

To say Clarity woke up in a tangle of limbs was an understatement, in such a relaxed state he realized that Calliope had several dorsal fins, and they were sharp and digging against Clarity’s side, they were effectively piled together like a pack of dogs. Was this how merpeople slept? Was it an ocean thing or just a Calliope thing? He wasn’t exactly sure, but he sure liked it.

He held onto Calliope like they were mated, meant for each other, he could pretend for a little while longer why the other slept. It must have been with the quickening of his heart that Calliope's eyes fluttered open, they rolled them a few times before focusing on Clarity.

"Oh, hello…"

"I didn't scare you that time?" Clarity tried to joke.

And for the first time since they met, Calliope smiled, soft and shy, but it was definitely a smile, "You assured me I was safe here. Perhaps I remembered such a thing in my sleep." he looked around the cave, "Is it morning? I can't really tell in here."

"Sure you can." Clarity offered, he pointed at the ceiling where slim, cone-like holes had worn out in the roof of his home. It allowed smoke to escape and a small view of the stars and moonlight. The sun was subtle and orange, telling him it was late in the morning. "Right up there, see? It must be getting close to noon."

"Noon?"

"Oh, when the sun is in the middle of the sky. But I bet you don't see that much do you. Do you ever surface?"

Calliope shrugged and made a face, "Not too often. Like I said, I'm not allowed to, but I don't wish to talk about that right now."

"That's okay there's no need to, I was just ya know, curious... Are you hungry? I think there's still some of that shrimp from yesterday."

"I hope I didn't offend you. My home life is simply troublesome."

"I get it. I mean I never even met my folks. They had me and dumped me. I don't think I was planned." Clarity said as lightly as possible, chewing shrimp as a distraction from Calliope's soulful and sympathetic gaze.

"That's terrible, how did you ever survive?" They asked, doing the same as Clarity,
eating slowly and thoughtfully.

"I scavenged is the best way to put it, I guess. That's how I know so much about humans and their shit. I stayed close to docks and riverbanks and found food, not too long after I found this place."

"Well, that's rather sad but this is a nice living quarters. I live in a cave as well, but it is underwater. A bit more confining. There's something odd and satisfying about letting your skin dry if only in the slightest."

Clarity laughed, "That is what you take from this? Not sleeping in as late as you want or no one nagging you. I'm gonna assume you get nagged a lot. I'm pretty convinced you're some kind of loyalty you'd just about have to be with the way you put things into words."

Calliope shifted themselves up onto their bottom, flattening out their dorsal fins to get more comfortable. "We are the largest pod where I live. I suppose that could be considered royalty. Sea folks, as you put it, come to my father for advice on an array of things."

"So you keep saying Dad, am I allowed to ask where Mom is?"

When Calliope frowned and shook their head Clarity only nodded in understanding, "I gotcha."

They stretched their tail out and shivered as they did so, finishing their meal and falling quiet for a few minutes.

"I'll go out and hunt today and bring back some more supplies. My friend Leddy I'll give her the rundown of what's going on so she can keep an eye out for any of you guys, that sound okay? Will you be alright if I leave for a while?"

"Of course," they nodded with a sigh, "I'm used to being alone."

Clarity wished he were able to dig deeper with this person, but they became so open and tightlipped at the same time it had his head spinning. But he could see it brimming on their face, that there was a lot more going on than just wanting to 'run away and nothing more'. "I'll be right back. I promise I won't leave you alone for very long." He took out a worn shoulder bag down and off a hook that held an array of human things he'd found over the years. He'd be gathering for two, so he grabbed the big bag.

~

He dove down through the opening in the cave and popped up into the hot air from the muddy waters. There were only two boats out today, not particularly busy thankfully. He'd have to search for Leddy; she hated boats as much as she hated people. So, when they were out and about she was sometimes hard to find. He was also keeping his eyes out for any more sea folks, he half expected a bunch of armed guards to show up with shields and tridents.

At least that was what he'd read in books or seen on screens from boats with TVs. There were even times that people would have picnics and use a giant sheet to display movies. He'd always hide behind the rocks and try not to draw attention. He supposed that was where he got most of his knowledge of human behavior outside of the water.

"Clar, what are you doing out again? You usually sleep until the evening when it's this hot." she was shielding her eyes against the blazing sun, "That sun is brutal. You still have your little bunkmate?'

"Yeah, doesn't seem like he feels like going home just yet. You know how we've always thought it's glamorous on the other side of the pond? Turns out it's not." He was collecting clams as he spoke, watching Leddy's hair flow around her like dark moss reminded him why he kept his own so short. It was just easier.

"Why? What's going on? Are there like shark people after him?'

"Led, that's just an old wives' tale."

"I don't know what that is," she growled, "Besides, it's possible. Just cause you haven't seen one doesn't mean they aren't out there. There was some in that movie you showed me. I mean yeah, they weren't people, but they were sharks and they got on land."

Clarity laughed, "Just because it's a movie doesn't mean it's true. Human's just like to make stuff up to entertain themselves."

"You mean like us?" she asked, raising an eyebrow.

"Set and point." he gave her the finger gun gesture that had her cocking her head, "Besides, they only seem to think that mermaids exist. Much prettier to look at."

"Please," Leddy laughed, "As if I'm worthy of their picture books. Besides, didn't you say your new friend was pretty?"

"Beautiful is more like it."

“You hope they stick around!” Leddy giggled beneath the water, bubbles fluttering above both their heads like minnows. “Somebody is in love.”

“Oh, for Argos sake I am not.”

“Please, it’s written all over your face, I can see it from here and it’s muddy too so you’re so smitten. You’ve been a loner ever since I’ve met you. You won’t even let ME go in your cave!”

“They’re just there until their head heals up and they find somewhere else to go. Why the hell would a sea dweller wanna shack up with a river tramp like me?’

She was still wiggling her eyebrows, “It’s like the perfect love story, isn’t it? Man, I wish those park idiots would play something besides romances. I think they’re starting to brainwash us.”

“You my friend, are ridiculous, I have to get back…” he said, securing the bag to his back, making sure the contents wouldn’t spill out once he started swimming.

She batted her eyelashes dramatically. “Hurry back to your love cove. If I find any more shrimp I’ll come by and knock.”

Clarity rolled his eyes, huffing loudly, blurring his vision with bubbles, “Sure, sure I’ll see you later.”

Leddy’s words were twirling in his head, the more and more he thought about it, the truer it became. How did he get so attached to someone so quickly? He wasn’t a human, that was a human thing, wasn’t it? He was actually excited to get back to his cave, not just to sleep, or hide from the boaters, no, he was excited for one reason. That made his heart do flip-flops, pretty typical he would fall for someone that was leaving. Story of his life.

His already turning stomach lurched when he saw Calliope sitting outside of the cave on one of the rocks, hand reaching out and seemingly admiring their flesh in the sun. The very intense sun.

“What are you doing out here?” he tried not to shout, securing his bag as he swam quickly to the cluster of rocks, “I told you to stay inside and shit look, now you’re sunburned! Didn’t anyone ever tell you about the sun burning you if you’re out too long? Especially given that you hardly surface.?”

Their eyes went wide and wet in that stupidly cute way, "I was simply curious about what it looked like outside. I didn't see anything, obviously, the other day. I-I'm sorry I didn't mean to anger you."

Clarity huffed, grunting as he pushed himself up onto the rocks beside the other merperson, "You didn't make me angry." He reached sideways and took their hand, examining the pinkish flesh. Every time he got close to the other, he was floored with how pale they were but it was a mother-of-pearl kind of paleness, it had a glow to it.

"You didn't make me mad, you just scared me. If you're really dead set on running away, putting yourself out in the open is a no-no. Not to mention there are humans around here. My cave here is far away from the parks and beaches but every now and again a human gets curious. I've had to get pretty creative a few times to scare them off. I don't want you getting hurt. And see?" He lifted their arm in front of their face. "You're pink now, that's sunburn, it's gonna really smart tonight."

They wrinkled their nose, "Smart? You inferred I was stupid."

"No," he shook his head, "Damn, you're kind of infuriating sometimes. No, I mean it's gonna hurt tonight. Might have to put some salve on it. I've got some somewhere, I think. You really haven't been above water much have you."

Meekly they shook their head, "Again I am very sorry for frightening you. I heard a noise and I followed it out. You were right about the boats. I saw one nearby."

"Did you hide?!" This time Clarity did shout and it made Calliope flinch.

"Behind the grasses over there." They pointed.

"Did they stick around?"

"They heard me splash, said some things, and then left."

Clarity took a breath, "Come on, let's get you back inside. No more exploring until you're 100% better got it?"

"Yes, I understand." He followed behind closely beneath the water and into the cavern.

“I’ll get the fire going again in a little bit. The embers keep this place nice and the heat of the day. But if you get cold you let me know cause I know for a fact you’re used to warmer waters than around here.”

This time Calliope smiled; it was slightly toothy as he nodded. “That is kind of you thank you.” It was interesting to watch them move on land, dorsal fins helping push against the rock until they were lying on the grass once more. “I’ve never felt anything like this, it smells much sweeter than kelp.”

“Eww, that doesn’t sound appealing at all. Sweetgrass is the way to go. Well, now we know where it got its name. I got you some clams. If you want, I could put them on the embers, and they taste different cooked.”

“You do many human things, don’t you,” Calliope said, eyes following Clarity as he moved around the living shelf. “I’ve never eaten cooked food and I’ve never been near a fire. I saw them from far away on an island once. But I thought perhaps it might be a trick of light.”

“Humans are a pain, but they have some smart things that I like to use. There aren’t a lot of merfolk around here and Leddy taught me how to hunt but that’s about it. I don’t even really know what she does on her own time.”

“Is she your mate?” They asked softly and with obvious hesitancy, their eyes focused on their long fingers braiding the grass in their lap.

For the first time all day that happy swelling returned to Clarity’s stomach, “No, she’s just a friend. I’ve never had a mate, have you? I mean that whole arranged thing doesn’t count in my opinion and also I think it’s bullshit.”

Thankfully Calliope giggled instead of becoming withdrawn, “No, I have found other merfolk appealing but never engaged in activities.”

“What are activities to you?” Clarity asked carefully.

“You know…” they waved a hand, “Kissing, touching…and mating.”

Clarity nearly choked on his own spit, “Okay, you know all about this stuff but not the sun? Besides, you’re pretty damn gorgeous not having a mate seems like a crime.” After he spilled the beans he felt his whole face go hot.

“That doesn’t seem so farfetched,” they began seriously, “You are beautiful and have had no mate.”

Holy shit they think I’m pretty. Which seemed ridiculous in his own opinion, “You’re just being nice. You’re like a fucking pearl and I’m…this….”

“What are you?”

“Muddy….” he wasn’t even sure why that was the first word to come to mind.

“And kind. You have nice eyes and coloring. I’ve never seen anyone like you, so I believe you are quite extraordinary.”

So floored by this admission Clarity had barely noticed the other had moved closer and had one porcelain hand in his hair examining without care. “And your mane is very soft…”

“My mane?” Clarity tried for a joke but the rest of it lodged in his throat.

Calliope’s hand slid down, through his hair, and then to the nape of his neck without even thinking Clarity moved his face sideways and pressed a kiss to the inside of Calliope’s wrist.

They gave a tiny gasp, and swallowed loudly, “What was that…”

“Umm, me being stupid?” he carefully took Calliope’s hand and rested it in their lap, “Let’s just eat huh? You’ve never had cooked food before, and I think that’s a shame so let’s just forget I did that and…”

Calliope quickly pecked him on the cheek, then returned to their space with a hurried scoot.

“Clams…right…” He cleared his throat, it was really hot in here and he felt dizzy. Color him surprised. He tried to erase the shocked look he knew was adorning his face. On the other side, Calliope was smiling, meekly and in that cute shy way but smiling like they were proud of themselves.

“Show me how to cook then…” they piped up, voice high and lyrical like some poetic image he’d usually scoff at.

~

Clarity decided that this was what it felt like to be in a family. They'd talked for hours after their supper, the remarkable difference of Calliope's home compared to Clarity. How land was a rare thing to see, as well as seagulls, animals with fur, and the multitude of colorful fish. Clarity had never seen a whale and Calliope had never seen a crocodile. They spoke like neither one would be leaving. A promise that either one would show each other their worlds.

Calliope wouldn't talk about their family, flat-out refused, and even became a little breathless when Clarity pushed. So the subject was pushed quickly aside and Clarity tried to remember more amusing stories of stupid humans. It didn't take long, and he had them laughing once more.

They fell asleep talking, tangled up like they had the night before. Like the innocent touch Calliope had given without thought, Clarity felt their fingers anchored in his hair and their face burrowed in the crook of Clarity's throat.

It was only when he finished his story of a group of pontoon frat boys, of their loud music, and eventually drunkenly falling off the edge of the boat had he noticed that Calliope had fallen silent, their hot, sleepy breath against his throat and snoring adorably. He held them close, closer than the night before, and nuzzled the top of their silver, glimmering hair, it smelled salty and crisp, almost flowery. He decided this would be his new favorite thing.

~

He was awoken by the shouting of his name, it echoed off the walls and bounced off the water. He groaned and held his charge closer, burrowing closer beneath the thick piles of grass.

"Clare!" the voice shouted again, "I don't know the way in, but I can see you in there. I need to talk to you NOW."

His vision was blurred when his eyes met the ceiling. "What?!" he instinctively shouted, but it was sleep-clotted enough not to shake Calliope awake.

"Not here, outside!" she whispered harshly, and then she disappeared.

It was difficult to untangle Calliope's arms from his torso, as well as make sure he didn't catch his scales on their dorsal fins that seemed to flex in and out when they breathed. He replaced his own body with more grass and slinked into the water to avoid making a splash.

His head broke the surface, and he came face to face with Leddy, "I saw a bunch of them."

"Who, fishermen?" he pushed his hair out of his eyes, coming out of the water so fast he was breathless.

"No, other seafolk, three or four of them and they were definitely looking for someone. Well, my guess is your new buddy…"

"Calliope, their name is Calliope."

"Well they looked angry." she hurriedly spat, looking over her shoulder, "They asked me if I'd seen anyone like them around and I said no. If I hadn't flashed my rock I think they would have gotten physical. Then they started making this weird noise I've never heard before…kinda like whales. It was pretty creepy."

"But they don't know where Calliope is? They didn't say their name?"

"No, but I'm not sticking around. I don't think they followed me, but I'd be careful."

A screeching sound, unlike anything Clarity, had ever heard permeated the water and air, the vibration of it had him and Leddy sinking. And then Calliope's voice between the sound, screaming.

"Come on," he grabbed Leddy's hand and pulled her towards the opening of his cave, he never led her through here and she'd never asked. They had spun around in circles, the silty grit of the lake clouding up their vision. A flash of glimmering white and Calliope still screaming. Then calling out Clarity's name with as much fear as the first day they met.

Amongst the flurry of white, Clarity thrust out a hand and held on when a body passed him. He and Leddy both were pulled back to the other side of the cave.

They were indeed seafolk and had their hands on Calliope but so did Clarity, he held on tight, they lost their grip and Calliope wrapped themselves around his torso, dorsal fins digging in sharply to hold tighter with a loud shout of "No!"

"You would be swimming around with this filth." One of them spat, both of them looked nearly identical, their complexion was different than Calliope's; they were a peachy color proof that they surfaced far more often. Their hair was pulled back neatly at the nape of their necks, in similar braids.

"What makes you all shiny and perfect?" Leddy growled, she'd take her place on his left side and he hoped that they looked threatening enough.

"Calliope is coming with us by order of his Father."

"I don't think so John Wayne…they aren't going anywhere they don't want to go. They've been missing for days and you're just now finding out where? Get the fuck out of here."

"I don't think you have the means to fight us," one of them said, so nonchalantly Clarity wanted to slap them.

It was then he realized that Leddy had disappeared from his side, and then chaos, there were rocks being hurled from every direction and within the madness, Clarity felt Calliope slip out of his hold. He sank into the water and pushed against the cavern to avoid the rocks, he could hear the guards screaming and throwing swears that echoed off the cove. When the lake quieted Clarity carefully resurfaced, he looked around to find everyone was gone, well, not everyone Leddy's head popped over the top of the cave, "You okay down there?"

"What happened?!" Clarity was in a frenzy, and Calliope was nowhere to be found.

"Did you like that I set a trap I had a bunch of rocks and used some of those stupid fishnets and dragged them up to the top? I really didn't get a chance to tell you it all happened so fast. Hey, where'd your friend go?"

Clarity began desperately swimming around the murky water, diving and rising, diving and rising, only finding the silt of the lake stirring up in his wake. Nowhere. They were nowhere. He'd failed to protect them as he'd promised.

"Ah, man, I'm so sorry. They must have snagged him."

For hours he searched every corner, every patch of grass and driftwood, and found nothing. He was resigned to return to his cave, alone, and feeling so sick to his stomach that he wouldn't eat for days.

~

The sunset and the moon rose many times before Clarity left the confines of his cave. He hadn't even built a fire; besides, it wouldn't kill him, it never got cold enough where he'd actually freeze. It had always been a comforting thing, now it only reminded him of what had happened and what he'd lost. Leddy brought him food, entering his home for the first time ever several times a day to check on him. And she did indeed care she just simply wasn't the lovey-dovey type. She'd pat him on the head and say it would get better.

But it didn't get better because he never knew what happened to Calliope, if they returned safely, got scared and got hurt, got lost, he just didn't know. He'd swam and searched for days. It wasn't until the brewing of a storm that he went outside, he sat on the muddy banks, pulling the sand up and over his tail. Despite his foul mood, he did enjoy the smell of a storm, the sky continued to darken, the rumbling in the distance was getting closer and closer.

He flopped down on the shore behind him, eyes on the clouds that began to swirl slowly and deliberately. He covered his eyes with both forearms and ignored the crash of thunder and a blinding bolt of lightning that filled in the crevices of his arms and into his eyes.

One drop, then two, then a dozen began pelting his face, he sat up and ran head first into something. "Ow! Goddamnit!" he rolled sideways into the thick mud and groaned, his vision nothing but spots for a few moments.

An accompanying "Ouch" coupled with his own lamenting. He forced one eye open and there they were.

Equally covered in mud, hair a tangled mess, skin a little more burnt, but turquoise eyes squinted and sparkling. "You're okay! Oh my God, I looked everywhere! Everything was just a shit storm!" he started but was tackled to the silty ground.

Those lips he'd felt on his cheek were now on his own, firmly, and desperate, swallowing up all the painful cries in his chest.

Calliope was here, in the flesh, pulling away and grinning ear to ear. They were an absolute mess for sure but looking elated, "It took me days, but I slipped away. T-There was one of those scaled creatures in the water and I led the guards to it where it was sleeping."

"You didn't feed them to a crocodile, did you?"

Calliope rolled their eyes, "No, of course not, I splashed around and screamed, and as devoted as they were to find me it scared them so bad, they think it ate me."

Clarity would have started laughing if he hadn't such a large knot in his throat, "So they just…didn't even bother trying to find you?"

They shrugged, "I stuck around. Hid and listened to them speak.

They both agreed they'd tell my father I perished in a great

reptilian fight."

"I'm not gonna lie, sweetheart, you and a croc? You'd never have a chance. You sure they won't come looking for you?"

"What is it that you said? We'll cross that bridge when we get there? I'd prefer that." and they dove back down and kissed him like it wasn't a foreign action at all. Virgin my ass, Clarity thought.

"That storm is getting rowdy, let's get inside. And…" he looked them over and laughed softly, "Let's get you cleaned up."

Calliope only grinned madly like a happy child and tackled him once more, wrapping their limbs up and around him as if they might become one. "I missed you."

"I missed you too." Clarity sighed; eyes closed in relief.

~

They hurried back into the cave as the wind began to pick up, throwing tree branches and beating the waves against the shore. It was all muffled inside the stone home. Clarity helped get all the twigs and mud out of Calliope's hair and digging in his array of human treasures he found a brush. For the first time in days, he started the fire up, the glow making shapes in scattered dances across the rock.

Currently, Calliope was laid out on their stomach, resting their head on their folded arms while Clarity combed their hair. Finally smoothed out and free of gunk it began to radiate that same light he'd seen the first day they met. "See, as soon as Leddy knows I can do this she'll never leave me alone.

“It feels wonderful, thank you. I don’t believe it's ever been this tangled.” They said, eyes closed and despite being happy, Clarity could see how utterly exhausted they were. “So…” they turned their head, little tendrils of silver falling across their cheeks. “You really don’t mind if I stay here?”

Clarity huffed an exhausted laugh of his own, he bent at the waist and kissed their cheek firmly before settling over their mouth. He gently pushed them to the grass, nuzzling the soft patch of flesh beneath their ear and wanting to bottle every adorable little moan that left their throat. Carefully he laid his body beside theirs until they were flush, hip to hip. He slipped one hand down the curvature of their back, resting his palm to the small of their back, the dimple of their spine. “Let’s face it. You only came back for my cooking.”

Calliope giggled and rubbed their nose on his cheeks, giving little kisses before they huddled into Clarity’s arms. The storm raged on outside, but all was quiet within Clarity’s new home, new safety, new happiness. He fell asleep with their huffy, happy breath upon his chest and made a list in his mind of all the things he planned on teaching them. Of all the things he’d discovered from the waves of a storm, this was the only time he ever felt like he belonged. Calliope was secure and safe in his arms, and the lapping of seawater and what it almost took from him far, far away.

In Seven Years

Robin Kelly

When her head broke the water's surface, she breathed in a lungful of cool sea air. She could see the shoreline, grey and bleak and windswept just ahead of her on the horizon. She followed the rest of her clan's lead as they swam towards the beach, which was illuminated by the last light of the setting sun. Before clambering onto land, she sniffed the salty air for any signs of danger. She couldn't pick up the scent of anything that could cause them harm. The beach was empty. Good. She lumbered onto land, her flippers slapping against the rough sand.

As the final seal reached the Irish coastline, without saying anything, slowly but surely, they all began to shed their skins. Greer followed suit, peeling off the tight, smooth skin that had cocooned her for so long. As she sat on the ground, she looked sadly down at the discarded seal skin, lying hollow and wrinkled on the sand.

Then she turned towards her clan and the elders who groaned and stretched their aching muscles. After years without the use of their limbs the children who had never before seen this form of theirs stared at their hands and feet in awe. She then gazed at her mother, whose long red hair now had flecks of grey in the strands. Greer didn't bother examining her own body, already knowing what her hands and feet looked like and that her own hair was a bed of unruly brown curls she would soon chop short. Instead, she turned to stare forlornly back at the sea.

Seven years.

Seven years it had been, exploring the depths of the ocean. Seven years of voyaging between distant islands. Seven years since she had walked on land with two legs. And now they were here.

Rather than sit there sulking, she stared down at her feet and wriggled her toes—time to stand. With a grunt, Greer hauled herself to her feet on shaking legs. She gazed downward and noted how the distance from her eyes to the ground had grown since last time. A growth spurt she only got to see the results of now. As she attempted to take her first step, she immediately fell flat on her face and ate sand.

She heard chuckling and raised her head. Being the first to attempt those bold steps, her fall had gotten everyone else's attention, and they were all looking at her. Heat rushed to her face, an unfamiliar feeling. She groaned and spat out cold, wet sand. Then she heard the soft padding of feet against the ground, and a hand appeared in her line of vision.

"It's alright, love," her father said, his voice hoarse from disuse. Greer hadn't heard it in so long. It wasn't that they couldn't talk in their other form, but they had little need to. "It takes a little while to get use to these land legs again." Greer ignored his hand and climbed to her feet on her own, determined to show she could do it by herself.

"Easy for you to say," she said, her own voice foreign to her, "you've been doing this forever."

"Not forever," he laughed, turning to face the sloped dunes before them. "But long enough to know what comes next."

Next, they had to rebuild. Fortunately, this was the part Greer actually liked. Between the ages of seven and fourteen, the last time she had lived on land, she developed the skills and fondness for building things. During this time, she had learnt from her parents how to build a house, furniture, and even the tools they would need to survive in these fragile bodies. She soon discovered her passion for carpentry, in particular, and started to make furniture for the other families within the clan as well.

This time they picked a spot of land not far from where they had first arrived near the coastline, not wanting to venture too far from the sea. Selkies were creatures of habit after all. Not far from the shore was a dense forest and though their homes were to be made of stone, the tall trees provided the lumber they would need. Greer ventured into the forest often, craving some alone time from her boisterous family. She would return with wood for their fires and for making tools. But most of all she liked to explore. Slowly, they built their settlement. The clan's elders chose it not only for its closeness to the sea but also to a nearby town. And while everyone else was anxious to explore the human town, Greer preferred the forest.

In her twenty-one years being alive, she found she much preferred her time as a seal over being a human. Humans were confusing and she didn't understand them. The complex nuances of social interactions, the unspoken rules of behaviour, the changes in other people's faces and tone of voice, and how they rarely said what they really meant, often alluded Greer. As seals, the simple calls and growls they used to communicate were far more favourable to her. Catching a fish in the sea came much more naturally to her than bartering for bread at a market. So, she stuck to the forest as one of the few places on dry land which she could truly understand.

~

Greer explored the forest on a cool, bright day, the gentle crunch of leaves beneath her feet. She had been working hard lately on making the tables and chairs for their homes and felt she had earned the break. As she ventured deeper into the woods, her ears picked up on the most unusual of sounds. It was a high, exciting sound, loud and repetitive as it bounced off the trees. She followed it, curious to know where it would lead. Finally, her journey reached an end, as she found a clearing just beyond the thick brush.

She peered beyond her hiding place and her eyes fell upon a girl. She was standing alone in the middle of the clearing with a strange stringed musical instrument, stroking it swiftly and expertly with a bow. As she did so, she tapped her foot and a wide smile spread across her face. Greer found it hard to look away, listening to the sweet, fast-paced tune.

She considered staying and listening to the melody but thought better of it. Sighing, she began to turn away. But as she did so her foot dislodged a loose rock and with a loud thump, she fell on her side. She groaned quietly to herself, annoyed by her own clumsiness. Suddenly, the music stopped.

"Who's there?" a voice called out. Before Greer could answer or hide, most likely the latter, she heard a rustling from the bushes and looked up to see the girl with the instrument standing before her. She brandished her bow like a sword, and pointed it towards her, while her other hand clutched the instrument tight.

"Ah, I surrender!" Greer cried, raising her hands. She didn't really feel threatened by the stranger's weapon of choice but didn't particularly want to get into it with her. The girl squinted her eyes as she stared at her. Greer quickly turned her gaze away from her eyes, instead, focusing on the bow in front of her, pointed inches from her nose.

"What are you doing back here?" the stranger asked. "Are you following me?"

"What? No!" Greer replied. "I just heard the music and followed it here. I was just leaving."

The bow seemed to move a few inches away, so Greer kept talking. "I'm in these woods all the time and I've never heard anything like that before."

"You're in these woods all the time?" the girl asked. "Then how come I've never seen you before? I live here."

"I'm new around here," Greer explained. "And it's also very hard to catch sight of me. I'm very stealthy." Then she heard a laugh, a bright, cheerful sound, and the bow moved away. Greer looked up and the girl was smiling at her. She felt the heat rise in her face.

"Clearly," she said. Tucking the bow under her armpit, she held out her free hand. "I'm sorry for, uh, threatening you just there. It's just you can never be too careful in these woods." Greer stared at the hand for a second and then took it and was hauled to her feet.

"I'm Fiona," the girl said, turning the helping hand into a handshake. "What's your name?"

"Greer," she replied, taking her hand back uncertainly. "I didn't realise any people lived in the woods. I thought all the people live in the town."

"Aye, I live here with my clan," Fiona said, pointing back in the direction she had come from. "We live in a clearing in the heart of the forest. What about you? Are you from the town?" Her tone changed slightly, suddenly sounding tense as a tightening rope.

"No, I live near the coastline with my family," Greer said. "I don't like the town. It's too loud and people always stare." Fiona nodded in agreement, some of her long black hair falling over her face.

"Exactly! It's far better out here. At least here I can hear myself think," she said. Then she nodded down to her instrument. "Can play this in peace too."

Greer hesitated for a moment, unsure of what to say. Then, before she realised what she was doing, she blurted out, "I liked your music!" Fiona glanced back at her. "Your song…it was good."

For reasons beyond Greer, Fiona's face seemed to redden slightly. "Thank you. Maybe you could come and listen again sometime," she said, before adding with another smile, "without falling over next time."

"I will do my best," Greer said very seriously. Fiona laughed again. Greer really liked Fiona's laugh.

"Fiona!" a voice suddenly called out from beyond the clearing. "It's time to come home!" Fiona turned in the direction of the shout.

"That's my brother Cian," Fiona said as she glanced back at her. "I best be off." Greer felt something like disappointment in the pit of her stomach. But then remembering what Fiona had said about meeting again, Greer felt new boldness rise in her. "Alright, until we meet again," she said with determination.

Fiona paused in her steps towards her brother's calls. She turned more fully to face Greer. "Until we meet again," she agreed.

~

After that day, Greer would come and meet Fiona at that same clearing, to listen to her play music. But after a while, it stopped being about that. Together they would hike through the woods, sharing stories about their lives. Greer would talk about living by the coast with her parents and Fiona told her about life in the forest with her brother. Greer sometimes talked about her past journeys to other islands and how she missed travelling around, of course skimming over the details of how her means of transport had been swimming across the sea.

In return, Fiona confessed she had never left her home and how she longed to see the world. She was also very understanding, compared to many other humans, and never judged Greer for not making eye contact or finding some social rules difficult. Eventually, Fiona trusted Greer enough to tell her that she wrote her own songs. At first, she said she was too embarrassed to show them to Greer. But over time, she began to play her own music. Sometimes she would even sing. She had a great voice.

Over that first year, they became close friends and Greer found that she was happiest when she went to meet the girl in the woods. For some reason, she found her far easier to talk to than any other person she had met in recent memory. It made her feel less lonely knowing her. But although she valued their friendship, she couldn't help but feel saddened that there was a part of herself that she could not share with Fiona. The part that belonged to the sea. But it wasn't long until she learnt that there were parts of Fiona that she hadn't shared either.

~

On a late summer evening as the orange light of the setting sun poked through the leaves of the trees, Greer set off through the forest to meet her friend. She had finished her chores for the day and not wanting to wait, decided to head off early to their meeting spot. Even if Fiona wasn't already there, she could relax by the water and wait for her. They had a new meeting place, by a lake they had discovered earlier in the summer. As she travelled to it, she decided to take the long route and pass by the old clearing where they had first met. But as she approached the clearing, she heard a new sound. It was not the sound of an instrument being played or a song being sung but of unfamiliar voices talking over each other.

"Now, are you both getting enough to eat at home?"

"You're not getting into any trouble with the elders, are you?"

"Love, I was just about to ask them that—"

"Well, you best wait your turn."

Greer's brow furrowed in confusion. The voices didn't sound threatening, but Fiona had once told her she could never be too careful in the woods. So, crouching down low so that she was hidden, Greer approached the clearing and hid behind a large oak tree. Darting her head out quickly, her eyes fell upon the strangest of sights.

Two large wolves were in the clearing, one sitting on the grass the other perched on a rock. Their heads were cocked towards each other and as they moved their jaws, exposing long lines of fearsome, jagged teeth, they continued to argue with each other. Greer almost fell back in surprise, but she braced herself against the tree trunk.

"Yes, Da, we're eating well enough and no, Mam, we aren't in any trouble." Greer was startled by the sound of an additional voice. It was the same voice that had shared stories with her and sang songs. Greer angled her head round the tree again, only for her eyes to fall on Fiona who was facing the two wolves. Next to her was a boy that looked rather like her. Greer guessed he must be her brother Cian. She froze, not knowing what to do. Should she leave? Should she let them know she was there? Something told her the right answer was not the latter.

But before she could make up her mind, her next move was decided for her as the wolf sitting on the rock sniffed the air and sprung to its feet. "Someone's here," it snarled, hackles raised as it bared its fangs. Suddenly, both wolves' heads snapped in the direction of Greer's hiding place. Oh shit, she thought instantly. The other wolf also stood and immediately tore straight towards the oak tree. Realising she was dead if she didn't do something, Greer scrambled out of her hiding place into plain sight and took off back the way she came.

"Wait!" she heard someone shout behind her, but Greer didn't stop running. Of course, she didn't get far. Wolves were much faster than people. If only they had been chasing her in the water. When she had her sealskin on. But things rarely worked out how they should. They caught up to her in a grove of ash trees and before she could consider climbing one, the two wolves were circling her.

"Who are you?" the bigger one demanded in a voice that was more of a growl, its tail swishing menacingly as it paced. "Are you a hunter, here to kill us?"

"What? N-no, I'm not a—" Greer frantically stammered trying to explain herself, though she wasn't sure what exactly she was meant to be explaining to talking wolves.

"A warrior then, here to harm our clan?" the other wolf barked.

"N-not at all! I don't even know how to fight that w-well," Greer stuttered, before realising that probably wasn't the right thing to say.

"Then who? Who are you?" The wolves stopped their circling and glared at her with fierce, gleaming eyes. It registered in Greer's mind that she was probably about to be their dinner.

"She's my friend!" a final voice cut in. All heads turned to see Fiona running towards them. Panting as she ran, she immediately put herself between Greer and the wolves. She was still huffing, out of breath, but spoke quickly, "She's not a hunter, she's my friend." Both wolves raised their heads, their ears flattening against their skulls.

They both seemed to exchange a look, before the smaller wolf spoke, "Fiona, she's not from our clan if I'm not mistaken. Do you have any idea how dangerous this is?"

"Yes," Fiona said. Her eyes darted back to Greer, before quickly turning to the wolves again. "But Greer is good. Yes…Greer is good." She nodded slightly to herself as she said it before adding, "And she's not from the town, she's from another clan entirely that just moved here from across the sea. If I explain to her, she'll understand."

One of the wolves sighed, which looked very strange indeed and exchanged a look with the other one. "Very well," it finally said, "but you must be very careful."

"I will." Fiona nodded, before turning to Greer. "Greer, this is my Mam, Deirdre, and Da, Conan!" She extended her hand to point to the wolves, a grin on her face which after knowing her for a year, Greer could only describe as frazzled.

"Oh, um, nice to meet you?" Greer said, eyeing the wolves with confusion.

"Nice to meet you too," the wolf, which Fiona had pointed out as her mother, said. "Sorry for hunting you just there."

"Yes, that was not a very good first impression at all," Fiona's father admitted.

"Oh, that's alright," Greer said, struggling to hide her bewilderment. "I would have done the same."

Conan barked out a laugh, before turning towards the edge of the woods where the boy who looked like Fiona stood. "Well, we best be on our way. Dangerous to stay in one place for too long," he said. His voice then dropped to something more serious as he addressed his daughter, "And remember. Be careful, Fiona." Then the two wolves and the boy disappeared into the darkness of the woods.

Greer turned to stare at her friend. Fiona let out a high, nervous laugh. "I have a lot to explain." Together they sat on the lowest branch of an old ash tree.

"I didn't realise I'd ever be explaining this to an outsider," Fiona said quietly. She then squared her shoulders and announced, "I am of the cursed clan from Ossory." She then winced as if expecting some big reaction.

Greer only stared at her, waiting for more information.

"Oh…have you not heard of us?" Fiona asked. Greer shook her head, not wanting to interrupt her with more words. Fiona then took a deep breath and explained, "Many years ago, our clan came upon a monk who cursed our people when we did not follow his ways. The terms of the curse were that two of our people would turn into and live as wolves for seven years before they were then replaced by two more. Right now, those two wolves are my parents."

Greer's eyes widened in astonishment. "What a strange curse." Fiona sighed. "Our clan has been trying to figure out how to lift it for hundreds of years, but no one has ever come close. It's a dangerous life, being a wolf."

"And do your parents live with you? In their wolf form?" Greer asked. Fiona's eyes cast downwards, and her hands clenched into the fabric of her dress.

"No, it was decided a long time ago that it would be too dangerous to hide two wolves in our home. They need to keep moving. Especially with hunters constantly searching for wolves to kill," Fiona said, with a bitter snarl that sounded just like her parents. Then her shoulders sagged, and her voice softened. "It's hard not seeing them. They've already been in this form for four years. I can't imagine having to wait another three to live with them again." Greer placed a hand on her friend's shoulder, not sure of what to say. Fiona looked back at her and smiled slightly.

Greer then asked the question which was on her mind, "Have you already been a wolf?"

Fiona shook her head. "Not yet, but my time will come." Then she eyed Greer, a look on her face that she could not decipher. "Why have you not run scared for the hills yet? Now that you know the truth surely you wouldn't want to be friends?"

At that, Greer actually laughed, realising that she and Fiona had more in common than she had initially thought. Of course, Greer's family had not been cursed. No, it had always been this way. Since ancient times, her people had always changed shape with every seven years which passed. Fiona stared at her wide-eyed as she giggled. She probably thinks I'm being very strange, Greer thought. Well, she shared her secret, might as well tell her mine.

"I'm a selkie!" Greer blurted out, without any lead-up, before sitting back to wait for her friend's reaction. Fiona's mouth hung open and for a moment she didn't say anything.

"Sorry, what?" she finally said.

"I'm a selkie," Greer repeated. "You know, a seal person. Every seven years me and my family transform from seal to human and then back again. Kind of like your clan, except it's all of us."

"Your whole family…" Fiona murmured. But then she blinked and exclaimed, "Wait, are you cursed too?!"

"No, not really." Greer shrugged. "It's always been like this. But I don't mind, I like being a seal."

"Of course, you do," Fiona laughed breathlessly, raking a hand through her hair. "Well, um, thank you for telling me your secret."

"Thank you for telling me yours," Greer replied and under the light of the rising moon within the grove of ash trees, the two friends smiled at each other, both knowing their secret was safe with the other.

~

Not long after they both had revealed their secrets, Fiona brought Greer to meet her clan in the forest. She got to meet Cian properly and found herself getting along surprisingly well with their clan. She then brought Fiona to her own home and introduced her to her parents Dòmhnall and Aileen. She also got to show Fiona the many things she had built and couldn't stop smiling when she admired her handiwork. Soon both clans began meeting and there were gatherings at night.

Fires would be lit and there would be dancing and drinking, and Fiona would play her instrument and sing, and Cian would sometimes play his harp. Greer didn't know how they could perform in front of people like that and one day, after she had expressed as much, Fiona visited, abruptly handing her a piece of vellum. Greer stared at the scrawl of messy handwriting blankly, unsure of what to expect.

"Um, I wrote this for you. You could sing it tonight. If you wanted," Fiona said very quickly. At that Greer blanched. She had never sung anything in public in her entire life.

"You don't want that," she warned her. "I'm a terrible singer."

Fiona rolled her eyes. "I'm sure that's not true." She then added more gently, "You don't have to if you don't want to. I just thought you might like to try."

Greer gulped. Recently she had started having other thoughts about Fiona. Not just of how smart she was, but of how pretty she was as well. How good it would feel to hold her hand or run her fingers through that long, dark hair. Knowing she had gone to the trouble of writing her a song certainly didn't help matters.

Greer quickly turned her attention down to the page and read the lyrics carefully, fully aware Fiona was watching. The lyrics hit her in a way that she did not expect. This song was about her. About them. After she finished reading it, she lifted her head from the sheet and stared off into the middle distance.

"Well?" Fiona asked, clearly not able to take the silence for much longer.

Greer turned to her and, with determination, said, "I'll sing it."

That night the two clans gathered at the fire for another evening of much needed revelry. Greer stared at the crowd before her, her nerves frayed, knowing she was sweating, feeling like running away, feeling like being sick. But then she looked at Fiona beside her, bow poised at the ready over her instrument, and she steeled herself and began to sing.

Though the sea is calling
And the cold wind blows
I dream of a place
Where the tallest trees grow
I linger in these woods
Hoping to go
Down the path back home
The path back home...

To Greer's relief, Fiona joined in for the next part and they sang together as their two clans clapped along. She felt her spirits bolster and her voice grew louder as she sang, filling the clearing with Fiona's song. When it finally ended, she was met with applause. She felt her face heat up and couldn't stop grinning. When she glanced towards Fiona she looked as happy as she felt.

Later that night after the party had ended and both clans had retired to their homes, Greer and Fiona stayed there, sitting with their backs to the campfire as they gazed up at the open sky, the pale light of the waxing moon washing over them.

"You did so well," Fiona said encouragingly. She then added, "'Can't sing,' she said. 'I'm terrible,' she said!"

Greer snorted. "Thank you, but I think I'll stick with carpentry."

As they sat together, she couldn't help but notice how pretty Fiona looked in the soft moonlight. She was suddenly overwhelmed with how badly she wanted to kiss her.

"You're really skilled," Fiona said softly. "I couldn't imagine being able to build anything."

Greer tapped her foot on the ground repetitively and stared off towards some trees, hoping to distract herself from the feeling building in her chest. "Mm," was all she replied.

Fiona only edged closer, placing a hand on her knee. "Are you alright?"

"Can I kiss you?" the words tumbled out of Greer's mouth before she could stop them. She had always been bad at keeping herself from saying exactly what she was thinking, but this was ridiculous.

Fiona paused—her brown eyes wide. Then, to Greer's surprise, she nodded slowly. Without saying anything the two women shuffled nearer, quickly closing the distance between each other. As their faces inched closer, they glanced at each other, both as excited as they were nervous. And then they kissed under the stars with the fire at their backs.

After that, the two women spent as much time as they could together. They were almost inseparable. Over the next few years, their bond only strengthened, and Greer found herself falling hard for Fiona. She had never felt this way about anyone before and when she admitted as much, Fiona confessed to feeling the same. But one day after almost three years since they had first met, Fiona asked to meet Greer by the lake.

~

She arrived to the sound of sniffling. Fiona was sitting with her back to her on a log by the water's edge, her head ducked low, buried in her hands. Greer felt the tension in her gut tighten in alarm, realising that something was wrong.

"Why are you crying?" she asked as she sat down beside her. Fiona raised her head, her hands dropping away from her face. Her eyes were red, and her face was pale as the moon. "Because it has just been announced. The seven years is coming to an end. Soon my mother and father will be human again."

"Well, that's good, right?" Greer asked, feeling confused at what could be the cause of her distress.

"Cian and I are to take their place," Fiona said, looking at Greer very seriously. "It's my turn."

Greer felt her stomach plummet at her words. They had talked about it before. What they would do when Fiona transformed, but she hadn't expected it to come so soon. She was at a loss for words, as her own head filled with thoughts too big to comprehend. After a moment she realised Fiona was still talking.

"—and I know that it's a long time to wait for someone, so I want you to know I understand."

"What?" Greer asked softly, unsure of what she had just missed.

Fiona took a deep breath and repeated, "I understand that while I am a wolf, we can't be together, that it's a long time to wait for someone, that you have to leave me."

"What? No," Greer said, taking her hands. "I'm not going to leave you over some silly curse. I'm going to help you!"

"But..." Fiona's eyebrows furrowed, "are you sure?"

Greer smiled at her. "I've never been surer of anything in my life."

~

Greer announced to her clan that she would be leaving their settlement and built a house of wood in the middle of the forest. Her family told her they were sad to see her go but understood why she was leaving. When the day finally came for the curse to be passed on, Greer was there in the clearing that was home to Fiona's clan. She stood by Fiona's side as she, her brother, and parents, and all the clan waited as the sun finally set. They shared a final kiss, tears in their eyes, as the last orange light slipped below the horizon, and Deirdre and Conan changed form from wolf to human. Then Fiona and Cian transformed, their human forms no more, as two large wolves stood in their place.

Crestfallen, Greer scrubbed at her eyes. The wolf with the darker fur stepped forward and nuzzled her hand.

So, Greer lived in her little house in the woods and, when they could, Cian and Fiona would visit. In those times that they came to her home, she would sit and talk with the two wolves for as long as they could spare, before they had no choice but to leave, cursed to continue their never-ending hunt. Before she would leave Fiona would lay her big head in Greer's lap, looking up at her with sad brown eyes, her ears flattened back as she let out a low whine. Saying goodbye was hard every time.

Living in the forest, Greer came to realise just how many hunters travelled through searching for wolves to kill. To protect Fiona and her brother, Greer would build and set traps in the woods. Nothing lethal, but enough to keep hunters away. But one evening, her traps did not go off and she saw two hunters edging through the woods with a huge wolfhound leading them in the direction of Cian and Fiona's current cave. Out of options, Greer quickly grabbed the spear she had been learning to use and raced ahead to cut them off at the mouth of the cave. They demanded she step aside, but she refused, standing her ground even as the large dog growled at her. Although she tried to explain herself, the two hunters would not hear it and one lunged out and attacked her.

Greer fought them with all her might but was soon overpowered. She landed on her back and only just raised her spear in time to block as one of the hunter's axes came down. The spear was splintered in half and as the hunter raised his axe again, a snarl ripped through the air and was followed by a blur of dark fur. The axe fell to the ground and Greer watched as the two wolves snapped at the hunters fiercely and sent them and their dog running out of the forest like the cowards they were. Fiona then ambled over and nosed at Greer's shoulder.

Greer offered her a small, grateful smile in return, comforted in the knowledge that as long as they were in these woods together, they would do what they could to protect each other. They were safe. At least, for now.

~

As the early evening light filtered through her windows, Greer sat in her small, cluttered kitchen, working on the finishing touches to a chair she had been building. As more time had passed, she had continued her work, making furniture that her clan sold in the town. At night she would sometimes hear the lonely howl of a wolf in the distance and knew that somewhere in the woods, Fiona was safe. As she was carving a small bird into the backrest of the chair, a knock on her door caused her to pause and look up.

She set down her tools and walked to the entrance to open it. There her father stood, a deep furrow to his brow and a regretful glimmer in his eye. In an instant, Greer realised that the truth she had been avoiding for the three years which she had been living in these woods could no longer be ignored.

"It's time to come home," he told her, sounding sad as he said it, "back to the sea."

Greer had never in her life been upset at the idea of returning to the ocean before. The promise of adventure as they travelled was exciting and the dark, cool depths of the sea were a comfort to her even with the dangers that came with that life. But now things were different. Now she had something on land she didn't want to let go of.

"Give me one more night with her," she said to her father, who nodded and placed a comforting hand on her shoulder. That night Greer told Fiona what was to happen.

"Tomorrow my clan will transform into seals once more and return to the sea," Greer told the wolf, in the warmth of her small wooden house.

"And then what happens?" Fiona asked.

"We will live in the sea, travel between the islands, and do what we have to, to survive the next seven years," Greer said, her shoulders slumping as a new feeling of hopelessness began to sink in. For the first time, she could understand why Fiona had told her to leave her all those years ago. She couldn't expect her to wait all that time for when she next resurfaced as a human. She frowned at the ground. "I suppose this time, this really is goodbye."

"I'll wait for you." Greer's head shot up and she stared at the wolf sitting in front of her. "I'll wait as long as it takes!"

"But…you don't have to, I told you I understand, you don't owe me any favours," Greer protested. She didn't want Fiona to give up her time waiting around for her while she lived in the sea. She deserved better than that. In four years, Fiona would be human again and she would be human the rest of her life. But Greer would always be changing from the form of a human to a seal and back again, every seven years for as long as she lived. Who could wait for someone like that?

"Since you have known me, you have done so much to help me," Fiona said, climbing to her feet. "You have been there for me no matter what form I have taken. Whether I was human or a wolf, you chose me. You are so full of love and kindness, and I am lucky to even have known you. Now let me return this kindness, my love. I do not feel that I owe you, I make this choice for myself." Greer was speechless as she stared at the wolf. She felt tears form in her eyes.

After a long moment passed, she nodded dazedly. "Alright." She laughed as the tears blurred her vision and Fiona nuzzled her hand.

The next day, in the early hours of the morning before the sun had risen, two wolves stood on the long stretch of beach and watched as Greer's clan made their final preparations. The selkies gave their homes to Fiona's clan, who thanked them for their kindness and generosity. Greer looked at the long, lonely grey coast. She remembered her first day arriving on this beach. How reluctant she had been to live on the land. Now she would do anything to stay. But the sea compelled them to return, they could not stay any more than Fiona's clan could lift their curse.

Just before the sun broke the horizon, Greer turned and wrapped her arms around Fiona's neck, burying her face in her fur. Then she heard her mother call out, "The sun is rising!" and together the selkies began to wrap themselves in their seal skins and transform. With a final glance towards the beach, towards Fiona, Greer donned her skin and as she fell to the ground, her flippers hit the sand and she was a seal once more.

She followed her family's lead as they lumbered towards the sea, the rising sun glancing off the waves. As soon as the cold water met her skin, she felt a rush of familiarity fall over her, like the feeling of returning home. But as she glanced back to the beach, her heart felt torn, realising that there were now two places where she felt she belonged. As she and the rest of her clan began to swim, she heard a single howl, which faded away the further she swam. And then she dived below the surface and was enveloped by the sea.

~

Living at sea wasn't so bad, there were just a few things Greer had to relearn. How to dive deep underwater, catch fish with ease and avoid orcas and boats. Her clan never travelled far at first, instead, swimming around the coast of the island they had come to know as home. Greer would sometimes return to that same beach they had left, hoping Fiona might be there. Sometimes before her head broke the water, she would hear howling and know Fiona would be waiting for her, still in her wolf form. As she reached the surface, she would be standing there on the coast, tail swishing back and forth. Greer would then lumber back onto the beach, and they would talk.

Those few moments they could steal together were precious to them and before they would separate, they promised to try and meet again soon. But before long it was time for her clan to move on, to find less treacherous waters, where they would be safer.

"Where will you go?" Fiona asked as they sat on the beach together on that final night. There were only three years left until she would once again be human.

"North, I think. Towards Orkney," Greer said sadly. "My clan knows that area well. Out there are more selkies for us to meet. There's safety in numbers after all."

"I will miss you," Fiona said. "I hope you and your clan stay safe."

"I will miss you too." They stayed on the beach together that night and in the morning, Greer returned to the sea to re-join her clan on their long voyage.

~

Travelling across the sea, the selkie clan encountered many dangers in the icy waters. Out in the open water were fierce orca which tried to eat them and ships of seal hunters who tried to catch them. There were many days in which the clan would have to go without food as they exhausted all their energy simply trying to survive. They swam between islands and would sometimes resurface and rest on a beach, hoping to find some solace, but this was often short-lived as their hiding spots were always found by hungry humans.

When the older selkies grew tired, Greer would catch as many fish as she could to help ease the hunger of her clan. She was constantly exhausted, and she missed Fiona with a deep ache in her bones, but she pressed onward knowing she had to help keep everyone safe.

They continued to travel north and finally reached the Orkney Islands. There, on one of the many islands, they did indeed find more selkies and they stayed with these seal-folk in their little cove, keeping each other safe from harm. There was still plenty of risk of hunters on the Orkney islands, as there was in many of the places they had travelled to, but the other selkie clan lived in a safe, secluded spot, far from human activity. They were grateful to this clan for helping them in their time of need. Even so, the next few years were long and difficult. Greer kept busy as much as she could, protecting both clans from danger, and tried to keep her mind from straying too often to woods that were dark and green.

~

One evening, Greer was out swimming in the sea alone, not far from the coast, searching for fish to catch. Suddenly, breaking through the surface of the waves was the smooth hull of a wooden boat. As fish scattered from all sides to avoid it, so did Greer, scrambling away as fast as she could. But she got caught in the current and pulled back towards the boat. Rather than fight it, she plunged downwards, putting distance between her and the water's surface. She then waited for the boat to continue on its way. Instead, it stopped.

Whiskers twitching nervously, Greer wondered why the boat had not moved on yet. Then she heard the strangest of sounds from above the surface. It was the sound of howling, but it certainly wasn't the wind. Curiously, Greer swam closer to the boat. The howling did not stop but only seemed to grow louder. It didn't sound like any animal she knew of. Instead, it sounded a bit ridiculous like a human trying to mimic the sounds of an animal. Suddenly, Greer remembered all the times waiting underwater to hear Fiona's howls from the shore. Her heart began to race. No. It couldn't be. Surely it cannot be her. But what if…?

Cautiously, Greer swam up and her head broke the surface of the water, poking up from under the waves so that she could stare properly up at the boat. Standing there on the deck, hands cupped around her mouth as she projected her howl out across the sea was a person Greer would know anywhere. It was none other than Fiona herself. She stared in shock at the woman standing on the boat, wearing warm travel clothes. She looked like an adventurer.

"Down here!" Greer called up to the boat. Fiona looked down and a grin spread over her face. She looked older now since Greer had last seen her in her human form. No longer the picture of a shy girl unsure of herself, but of a seasoned explorer ready for adventure. It suited her.

"There you are!" she called down to her. She then turned and yelled behind her, "Cian, get the plank!" A plank was then lowered into the water allowing Greer to clamber over it and onto the deck of the boat. There she saw not only Fiona and Cian, but a motley crew of other members of their clan. Suddenly, she felt two arms wrap around her neck and she was being hugged once again by the love of her life.

"I can't believe it! We finally found you," Fiona cheered as she kneeled before Greer. "I thought it would near take forever. You know there are a lot of islands that make up Orkney, Greer!"

"I can't believe you're here," Greer admitted in a daze. She had never imagined Fiona would come all this way. "Where did this boat even come from?"

"I built it!" Fiona said excitedly. "With the help of my clan, of course. We took a page out of your book and built this boat ourselves. Took a long time to get it right, but we got there in the end."

Greer couldn't believe it. Fiona had learnt how to build a boat. For her. If seals could cry, she would be sobbing. "I can't believe it. You came all this way for me?"

"Of course." Fiona nodded. "Took a while to find you, but we just followed the rumours of selkies going round the islands to this one. Folks can be so superstitious." She said this last part with a wry smile.

Greer still couldn't get over her shock. She knew that Fiona had said she would wait for her, but she didn't realise that entailed building a boat and venturing across the sea to be with her. "I still don't understand…" Greer said, feeling overwhelmed.

"I told you," Fiona said with a gentle smile, "I'll wait as long as it takes."

So, Fiona and the rest of the crew aboard The Sea Wolf docked their boat by the cove and greeted the two clans of selkies. They stayed on that island, protecting the selkies by warding off approaching ships and keeping seal hunters away. In return, the selkies kept the crew fed with the plentiful fish they caught. Greer couldn't remember the last time she had felt this happy.

~

Greer swam as fast as she could, racing the setting sun, in the direction of The Sea Wolf floating on the water. She had to get on board as soon as possible. The boat had sailed just slightly out from the coastline and the crew were keeping a vigilant watch on this most important day. Three years had passed since the boat had first made its way into this cove. Three years since Greer had been reunited with Fiona. And finally, today was the day. Her father had approached her earlier that morning and told her the news. As soon as the sun set, they would be human once more.

As Greer swiftly swam towards the boat, she recalled the last time she had done this. How sad she had been, standing on that dreary beach, her seal skin lying vacant on the ground. But that was a long time ago and things had been very different back then. Now as the plank was lowered and she climbed onto a solid surface, her flippers hitting the boards, she had something to look forward to. With Fiona smiling at her, waiting patiently, Greer wrestled out of the seal skin as quickly as she could.

She climbed to her feet hastily and just like every time before this one she stumbled and almost fell to the ground. But this time Fiona was there to catch her. A blanket was then thrown over her shoulders and Greer got her balance and stood up on shaky legs. And as a thirty-five-year-old woman standing aboard a boat that was destined for many adventures to come, Greer did not have to choose between the sea and being with her partner. The open ocean now called to the two of them.

She smiled at Fiona, who smiled back in return, and she looked so beautiful, her black hair curled by sea spray and her lovely face a ruddy red. Her heart pounding in her chest, Greer leaned forward and for the first time in ten years, she kissed the love of her life.

Angel Eyes
Lynette S. Hoag

By moonlight, fairies conduct the dangerous, endless business of gathering food, fuel, and other materials necessary for living. They were six in number: Kookie, Jimi, Nam, Jin-Dee, Nightingale, and Honee. All males were passionate and companionate bonded pairs: Kookie with Jimi, Nam with Jin-Dee, and Honee with Nightingale. They lived in relative harmony as a hive mind, occupying a hollow tree home they called Euphoria. They carefully avoided excessive emotions and conflict and, therefore, were generally content.

Born and bred in a premier laboratory in Korea to sing, dance, and entertain, the fairies performed for wealthy patrons worldwide for many rotations around the sun. However, on a trip to America, the canny fairies escaped The Handlers. They had been indentured to The Handlers all their lives. Required to practice, perform, and conform to an endless loop, forbidden to speak English, though they were required to learn it. They were not so much enslaved as simply not free to make a single decision about any aspect of their lives.

However, their Creators and The Handlers did not realize the musical brilliance for which the fairies were bred and hand-selected, translated into real-world intelligence. After "The Escape," through perseverance, wit, and a bit of luck, the fairies had managed to forge a life on their own in a sanctuary forest near a small suburb outside of San Diego, California. They vowed to speak English instead of their native tongue, Korean. This was primarily as a dig at The Handlers but also a sign of the new life they chose to live.

Tonight, outside the hollow tree home, Euphoria, two of the six fairies gathered food scouted earlier in the day. Always cautious, Kookie was on lookout duty while his bonded mate Jimi gathered wild rice near the sanctuary's stream.

"Hurry Jimi," Kookie urged, "it is creepy out tonight. True? We do not like it." Kookie looked around feeling nervous. He flung his pink bangs out of his emerald eyes, reflexively.

"We are done and, on our way, back . . ." Jimi stopped short of finishing the sentence. "Kookie! Come quick! There is a fairy here, and he is hurt." Jimi was halfway between the hideaway and the stream, arms full of the wild rice he had bagged. He dropped the rice and swooped down to the ground.

"Be careful Jimi. It could be a lure." Though he had just counseled prudence, Kookie rushed over where Jimi landed. He spied the wounded one lying in a heap on the ground, a complication of iridescent wings, pale skin, and black hair. He squatted down next to the injured fairy and touched his cheek. It was dirty, clammy to the touch. "He is still breathing," Kookie said.

"We have to help him!" Jimi fretted. "If we do not, he will die."

The foundling was laying on his side, naked, his black hair tangled and matted. He had visible cuts and scrapes. His shimmering, fragile wings were crumpled.

"He is not one of us Jimi. He could be a lure back to The Handlers. True? They know we are soft-hearted."

"If we do not help other fairies, then who will help us?" Jimi complained.

Kookie looked into Jimi's violet eyes. They had been bonded many rotations and rarely had to verbalize the end of any sentences. Kookie could sense the emotions behind Jimi's eyes, and he did not like the feeling.

Kookie sighed. "Okay, for now. But we must be cautious."

It was not hard to lift the injured fairy, so Kookie picked him up in a fireman's carry and flew him into the hideaway. Jimi was close on his heels, carrying the wild rice.

There was not often drama in Euphoria. A new fairy arriving at the hive via Kookie's shoulder was the most exciting thing to happen in at least a rotation. Because they were a hive mind, everyone felt Jimi's excited panic the moment he found the injured fairy, but they had no idea what caused the panic. All activity stopped when Kookie entered the tree, and everyone rushed down to greet them.

The space inside the tree was bright, lit up by phosphorescent minerals affixed to the trunk from top to bottom in columns. Colorful flowering vines climbed up the inside of the tree giving it an elegant look and delightful scent of jasmine, honeysuckle, and wisteria. Giant wood ear mushrooms sprouted intermittently up the interior. Each mushroom was decorated with multi-colored leaves and flower petals. The mushrooms served as beds, couches, or just a hangout.

Kookie placed the wounded fairy on the empty mushroom bed reserved for treating the occasional injuries suffered in their wild outdoor natural existence. It was nearest to the entrance and easy to access. Kookie and Jimi were joined by the other bonded pairs, Nam and Jin-Dee, Nightingale and Honee, to assess the condition of the pale, semi-conscious foundling lying naked on the bed before them. The fairy opened his eyes in response to the attention. He shifted from his side to his back and blinked his eyes in the light. "Eeeeyeee," he cried out, then coughed before slipping back into semi-consciousness.

"That is a good sign," Jimi said, brushing his shoulder-length blue hair out of his eyes and placing a hand on the injured one's arm. "He has the life energy to heal."

Kookie felt shy staring at the hurt fairy's nakedness. His eyes kept being drawn to the foundling's perfect, pink manhood, ample for his size. He should decide if we look at him in this way. True? He went in search of bedding and sleeping clothes. When Kookie returned, he put the blanket over the injured fairy and stashed the sleeping clothes for later use. Then the fairies of the hive took stock of both the features and injuries of their new ward.

"His black hair and sable eyes make him look like an angel," Nightingale remarked as he reached out to stroke the tangled mass of waves surrounding the fairy's face. "We have never seen such lashes! We vibe with it. We must call him Angel Eyes until we find out his true name." He giggled with tender affection.

“He is not so spectacular,” Honee, Nightingale’s bonded mate, said. Honee had dark blonde hair, braided into a single braid that hung to his knees. He held the end of the braid in his fingers and studied it with his citrine eyes. He felt a twinge of jealousy that Nightingale was fascinated with the injured one. He wished that Nightingale was touching his braid right now instead of Angel Eyes’ hair. He vowed to kiss Nightingale’s head, full of strawberry red locks, over and over and tell him how beautiful the color was, tonight, as they mated. He would hold Nightingale’s turquoise eyes with his and make Nightingale scream his peak.

“Oh. Cool. Okay. He is singular,” Jin-Dee agreed, running his hands through his own wild purple hair. “He is small, precious like a baby bird. We want to protect him.” Jin-Dee touched the wounded fairy’s hand, curled into a tight fist.

Nam shrugged his shoulders. “We agree with Honee. He is not so spectacular. Jin-Dee is much prettier than this fairy. Jin-Dee’s purple hair and moonstone eyes are exceptional. There is none like him.” He leaned in and nudged Jin-Dee’s neck with his nose. Then took an obvious deep breath, inhaling Jin-Dee’s scent. He whispered in Jin-Dee’s ear, “Jin-Dee is the fairest of them all. Tonight, when you reach the peak, it will be only for Nam.”

Jin-Dee blushed deep, then a smile lit up his moonstone eyes. He nudged Nam back with his nose.

The fairies of Euphoria had many similarities: Iridescent wings, dark lashes, plump pink lips, contrasting with their peaches and cream complexions. They also shared delicate features and perfect white teeth. Their hair and eyes were various pastel and primary colors. This was by design. They were created in a lab, bred to be breathtakingly beautiful, musically inclined, and physically fit. The fairies were also selected because of their chemistry as a performing group. The bonus come along traits were cooperativeness, emotional coolness, and drama avoidance, for the most part.

Taking in the appearance of the foundling huddled under the blankets, they noticed his physical differences first. He was smaller than the smallest of them by a few centimeters. While they had picture-perfect teeth, he had mildly elongated canine incisors on the top and bottom and a chipped front tooth. They had bright pastel-colored hair and eyes. Angel Eyes had wavy black hair and dark eyes. Their black lashes were straight, his were extra-long curling upwards to his brows, the end of each eyelash dotted with a miniature black daisy flower.

He shared their other similarities, however, peaches and cream complexion, plump pink lips, delicate features, and iridescent wings. All agreed on Nightingale's nickname and called him "Angel Eyes." At least until they could find out his actual name.

"He has elongated canines. Maybe he is a little bit faerie. True?" Kookie surmised as he studied Angel Eyes' mouth and teeth.

"Yes. Faeries are chaotic, evil, and engage in malicious mischief," Nam said. "He will bring much discord to the hive if he is faerie."

"But he looks like us . . . mostly." Jimi shrugged, caressing an errant strand of his shoulder-length blue hair behind his ear. "We are just guessing from the appearance of his teeth. That is not fair."

"Angel Eyes is already causing conflict," Honee said. "We do not often fight and disagree, and we are fighting because of him. Angel Eyes stirs our emotions for reasons we do not know. When he gets well, he should leave and find his own faerie folk."

Jimi pouted. He was already irrationally attached to the feral creature, shivering beneath the fuzzy blanket. "But if he does not bring evil chaos, he can stay?" Jimi ventured.

Kookie sighed. "We will see." He stroked Jimi's arm.

The immediate problem with Angel Eyes was that his fragile wings were crumpled, hampering flight. Iridescent wings were slow to heal, even with the best care. He was also filthy, naked, with visible cuts and scrapes on his face, arms, and torso. He was probably hungry too.

"We should divide the care tasks," Kookie said.

"Oh. Cool. Okay. We will make healing ointment, porridge with medicinal herbs and warm honey wine," Jin-Ddee volunteered himself and Nam. Nam nodded in agreement, happy to escape the intrigue surrounding Angel Eyes. They flew off to the kitchen area together holding hands.

"We will do his hair," Nightingale volunteered, his hands still stroking Angel Eyes' dark tangled waves. "Honee, get us scissors, a comb, and flower shampoo, please."

Honee reluctantly peeled off from the group to search for the items, his mind racing; his thoughts troubled. Angel Eyes is faerie. He is making Honee unhappy with Nightingale. We are never unhappy with Nightingale.

Jimi and Kookie secured clean, soapy water in a hand-hewn bucket and sat on either side of Angel Eyes. They dipped flower petals in the water and cleaned his body and its wounds of dirt. Jin-Dee and Nam returned with healing ointment, honey wine and porridge with medicinal herbs. Jin-Dee carefully traced Angel Eyes wounds with the ointment, leaving flower petals as bandages over the deeper cuts on his arms and gouge in his right foot. Jin-Dee and Nam turned Angel Eyes onto his stomach, carefully spread his wings and Jin-Dee applied healing ointment to the crumpled extremities. Nam sat on the bed and watched every move of his purple-haired mate as he ministered to Angel Eyes' wounds. Maybe Honee is right, Nam thought as he watched Jin-Dee care for Angel Eyes. Angel Eyes is stirring negative emotions. We feel jealous that Jin-Dee is touching Angel Eyes. We have not felt this way in many rotations. Nightingale tried his best to comb the knots out of the tangled hair after cleaning it. He could only get the wavy bangs unknotted. He reluctantly scissored off the rest of the hair close to the scalp. He left the bangs hanging long over Angel Eyes' forehead, just skirting his dark eyes like Kookie's did.

After Angel Eyes was cleaned, bandaged, and dressed in sleeping clothes, Jimi set him up in the bed. The foundling roused, opened his eyes, and fixed them on Jimi. Jimi gave him sips of warm honey wine until he spit out a little. He laid back down and Jimi pulled the blanket up under his chin. Jimi turned to the other fairies. "We will take the first watch. Sleep tonight. We are sure there will be much to do in the future to take care of Angel Eyes. That is fair."

“We will stay with you,” Kookie said, running his hands through Jimi’s hair.

“Goodnight, Jimi and Kookie,” the remaining fairies said in unison, then headed in pairs to their bonded beds.

As soon as they landed on their bed, Honee put his arms around Nightingale, smelled his hair then ran his fingers through the strawberry-colored strands. “Nightingale is the most beautiful fairy in the world,” Honee said, eliciting giggles from Nightingale in response. He rubbed Nightingale’s nose with his.

“And Honee is the sweetest,” Nightingale said.

Honee and Nightingale had not been each other’s first choice for bonded mates when the bonding rituals began in captivity. But the first time they mated, their chemistry was explosive, undeniable, vigorous. Honee loved Nightingale’s gleeful, bouncy, personality that included frequent hugs, cuddles, and opportunities to kiss his elegant erection. Nightingale loved Honee’s sweet steadiness, sexy body, and even his moody pouting. Most of all, he loved the way Honee kissed his manhood until Nightingale reached his peak. Honee undressed Nightingale and pushed him onto his back on their bonded bed. The hive agreed, Nightingale had an absolute picturesque hard-on. The shaft was alabaster, straight, thick, and stood in perfect proportion to rose-pink testicles. It reached to his navel and begged to be kissed. Honee gazed at the naked glory of his mate. Nightingale wrapped his legs around Honee’s waist. Honee pulled the cover over them and took Nightingale in his arms.

Above them on their bonded bed, Nam and Jin-Dee knelt in the middle of it facing each other. Nam gazed at the uncommon exquisiteness that was Jin-Dee. He kissed Jin-Dee's fingers then moved to his lips. “Jin-Dee,” he whispered inches from Jin-Dee’s mouth. Then said again “Jin-Dee,” just before he kissed his lips. Jin-Dee caressed Nam’s face, his thumb hesitating over the dimples on each side of Nam’s full lips. He ran his fingers over Nam’s green buzz cut. “Moon-ah,” he whispered his Korean pet name for Nam. “Saranghae . . . we love you.”

When Nam met Jin-Dee for the first time, he was completely smitten. He'd fallen hard, like an angel without wings pushed from heaven. When he struck the ground, his soul shattered into millions of shiny pieces all etched with Jin-Dee's name. There was nothing else. Not time. Not space. Not heaven. Not earth. There was only Jin-Dee. But Nam was not alone in his obsession with Jin-Dee. Everyone wanted beautiful, oblivious, guileless Jin-Dee. Everyone. When the bonding rituals began all the fairies made a play for Jin-Dee. Nam felt insecure, like just another crush.

So, Nam had a furtive, one-night, encounter with Nightingale, who wanted Nam as much as Nam wanted Jin-Dee. It wasn't Nam's intention to mate with Nightingale that evening. He had rolled out of bed in his flannel pajamas for the meeting. But Nightingale was dressed to seduce. He wore a dancer's tank and close-fitting silk boxers. His strawberry-red locks were in his face, and he was flushed with desire. Nam slid up the tank until he could see Nightingale's lower abs. He touched the soft skin of his stomach, saw Nightingale's perfect, erect member peeking over the top of his silk boxers in the dim light of the hallway. He caught Nightingale's bewitching scent. When Nightingale's lips met his, the heat transfer between them set Nam afire. Nightingale's desire for him was real. Palpable. Affirming. He and Nightingale snuck outside, away from the view of the cameras, and shared an unforgettable moment of passion that ruined Nightingale's silk boxers.

A few moonrises later, Jin-Dee, the only fairy that mattered in Nam's universe, turned his doe-eyed gaze in Nam's direction and never blinked. After Jin-Dee confessed he loved Nam too, the sexual tension between them was so strong, The Handlers were forced to move up the bonding ceremony. Jin-Dee had to be "taken off the market" and firmly placed in an officially sanctioned, bonded relationship with Nam. Otherwise, a large-scale sexual revolution of rogue mating would threaten the tightly controlled environment.

The Handlers insisted the performing fairies keep their emotions checked. Emotional outbursts were perceived as “unrefined” and punished severely. Bonding was only allowed because it kept the fairies' sexuality controlled. Crushes were not tolerated and expressions of love between bonded pairs were only allowed in limited amounts. In captivity, even after Nam won the glittering title “Officially Bonded with Jin-Dee” he was afforded precious few moments to mate with him.

Each time Nam lay Jin-Dee on his back on their bonded bed in the hive, kissed his fingers, his lips, his neck, and stared into his moonstone eyes, he remembered the nights when he slept alone, aroused, full of unspent passion with only one wish, Jin-Dee. Tonight, was no different. Nam pulled off his shirt, never taking his eyes from Jin-Dee’s. “Jin-Dee is the fairest of them all,” Nam said as he took Jin-Dee’s lips in a deep kiss. “Say ‘Nam’ tonight when you reach your peak.”

“We will say Moon-ah. Again and again,” Jin-Dee promised as he put his hand on the back of Nam’s neck, drawing Nam back on top of himself on the bed. “Again and again.”

~

On the invalid fairy’s bed, Kookie and Jimi slept on either side of Angel Eyes. Well, tried to sleep. Angel Eyes moaned in his dreams and, at times, made weeping noises. Around midnight he sat up and said a single word, “Hungry.” His voice was unexpectedly rich and deep. Angel Eyes repeated ‘hungry’ insistently until Kookie roused, rose from the bed, and located the now cold, medicinal porridge.

Kookie handed the porridge to Jimi. “We will warm up more porridge and some honey wine, just in case Angel Eyes is still hungry.” He flew to the kitchen.

A drowsy Jimi sat in front of Angel Eyes with the bowl of cold porridge and Angel Eyes opened his mouth to be fed. Jimi smiled at the trusting innocence of it and fed Angel Eyes spoon after spoon of cold medicinal porridge. Angel Eyes looked into Jimi’s eyes with each spoonful, intensely studying his face until Jimi felt shy. When all the porridge was gone Angel Eyes said softly, “Hungry.”

“We are here with more,” Kookie landed on the bed and sat with another bowl of porridge and honey wine. He handed the wine cup to Jimi and Angel Eyes opened his mouth. Jimi held the cup to his lips until he drank his fill, then continued by spooning the warm medicinal porridge into his mouth. Angel Eyes rested his clammy hand on Jimi’s knee.

When all the porridge and wine was consumed, Angel Eyes smiled at Jimi and looked over to Kookie yawned and said, “Sleepy.” He lay back between the two fairies but reached for Jimi’s hand. Gripping the fingers tight he fell back asleep.

“The healing ointment is working,” Kookie said.

“Yes. Sleep tight Kookie our love,” Jimi said.

“Sleep tight Jimi our love, and do not let the Angel Eyes bite,” he added to their mutual amusement and snickering.

~

The morning sun rays peeking through the air vents in the tree found all the fairies once again seated around the mushroom bed containing Angel Eyes. Watching. Waiting. Wanting to know more. He squirmed under the covers and finally released Jimi’s fingers. He yawned, stretched then sat up in the bed, eyes wide with panic.

“Where is Taye?” Angel Eyes looked frantically around the group of fairies.

“What a deep voice,” Nightingale said. “Deeper than any of ours. We vibe with that.”

“Where is Taye?” Angel Eyes repeated and bit his thumbnail nervously.

“Who is Taye?” The hive asked in unison.

He pointed to himself. “Where is Taye?” His chest heaved with the threat of tears. Where is Taye?” He asked again. The tears flowed, caught on the daisy flowers at the ends of his lashes, and hung like droplets of rain before they spilled over onto his pale cheeks.

“Do not cry,” the fairies said in unison, moved by his emotion.

“You are safe, here with us in Euphoria. Our home. We will take care of you until you are better. Even longer, if Taye needs it,” Kookie said as he wiped the tears that splashed down Taye’s cheeks. “You are welcome here.”

Jimi reached out to stroke his freshly cut head, then pushed the mop of bangs out of Taye's eyes. "We will not let anything hurt you," he promised. "We will be fair with you."

Taye began gasping for air as the tears flowed. He wailed inconsolably and all the fairies took turns holding him in their arms, singing soft songs to him in Korean, and wiping his face. When he finally stopped wailing, he began sucking on his fingers and rocking himself. Jimi put his hand on his shoulder and asked, "What is wrong now, Taye?"

"Taye is of age. But Taye has not mated. Taye is not bonded. All that Taye knew is gone." Fresh tear drops clung to the tips of his daisy lashes.

Jimi took his hand. "Taye can mate with Jimi when Taye is ready," Jimi said as he kissed Taye's hand.

"Taye can mate with Nightingale when Taye is ready. We vibe with Taye," Nightingale said as he stroked Taye's head.

"Oh. Cool. Okay. Taye can mate with Jin-Dee when Taye is ready," Jin-Dee said. "Taye is a singular beauty."

"Yes. Taye can mate with Nam when Taye is ready," Nam said.

"Taye can also mate with Honee, if he wants to," Honee added with a shrug.

Kookie took Taye's other hand, "Kookie will mate too, if Taye so desires. Taye can bond with any of us and make us a bonded pair of three. True? Whenever Taye is ready. If that is what Taye wants."

Seemingly reassured, the exhausted fairy lay down on the bed, still clinging to Jimi's hand. "We like that," he said. "Sleepy." Jimi covered Taye with the blanket using his free hand.

"We guess we are staying here the day," Jimi said, indicating the grip Taye had on his hand.

"It is okay," Kookie said. "We will do your chores." He kissed Jimi on the forehead and then reached over and gently stroked Taye's hair.

~

When the fairies returned to the hive mid-day, the air was charged with feral sexual energy. Kookie could feel Jimi's arousal like his own, but this wasn't just Jimi's arousal. After stowing the food and fuel gathered, everyone went to check on Taye and Jimi. Taye slept on his back, still clinging to Jimi's hand, his erection visible through his pajama pants.

"Oh! He is ready to mate. We vibe with that." Nightingale giggled.

"It seems. But he would not touch his arousal or let Jimi touch it. Taye said he is scared," Jimi informed the group.

"We will wait then, for his wet dream. Hopefully it will be soon, and we will not all be constantly aroused for many moonrises waiting for him to reach his natural peak." Kookie added.

~

That night as Taye slept between Jimi and Kookie, he began to moan quietly in his sleep. The moans slowly increased in volume and intensity. He rolled onto his back and arched it. "Ah. . . ah . . . ah." His soft cries are like the opening verse of a hymn. He writhed as his body gradually climbed to its peak and his cries crescendoed. He gasped out "Eeeeyeee" and panted his release, still sleeping, fingers in his mouth.

"Thank the heavens." Jimi and Kookie thought.

~

Over the next few moonrises, Taye healed enough to sleep alone, affording Jimi and Kookie the opportunity to mate. They sat on their bonded bed, aroused and kissing.

"Kookie will mate with Jimi tonight?" Jimi whispered in Kookie's ear.

"Yes, our love. Yes." Kookie said, tracing the outline of Jimi's lips with his forefinger and caressing an errant strand of blue hair behind his ear. "We have missed mating with you. You are much aroused from sleeping with Taye on his sick bed with his unending erections. True? He has us all going with his unmated eros."

"You will forgive Jimi for peaking fast tonight?" he said as he pushed Kookie onto his back and grabbed two handfuls of Kookie's pink hair and took his lips in a fierce kiss as he mounted his mate.

"Yes. Yes." Kookie gasped as he felt Jimi's erection slide against his. "Oh, yes and we will mate again our love. Tonight."

In a world of carefully cultivated beauty, Jimi and Kookie were a water droplet of perfection. If you split it, both drops were the same. And just like a droplet of water, when it became one again, blended seamlessly as if it never were apart. They were evenly matched in their talent, abilities, and handsomeness. There was nothing either could not do. They could dance, sing, and charm any wealthy patron with their flawless looks and physiques. It did not seem, to the other bonded pairs, that Kookie and Jimi were even aware that jealousy was an emotion. No one, it seemed, had anything they desired. When they met each other, the attraction was mutual, immediate, and unconditional. Their talent and bewitching aesthetic afforded them frequent opportunities to mate with others, which they took. But nothing broke their bond; nothing stirred emotional strife between them. Not even a feral, exotic, aroused fairy with the eyes of an angel.

~

As expected, Taye's wings were slow to heal. He also had a large gash in his right foot that was still sore and caused pain with walking. Taye was stranded in the bed for the duration of the day and still needed help with his activities of daily living. Just as Jimi predicted, there were enough chores concerning Taye's care, and keeping, to go around.

This morning it fell to Jin-Dee and Nam to care for Taye. Jin-Dee sat on the bed watching Taye sleep. He resisted, then gave in to the urge to brush Taye's bangs over his forehead and out of his eyes. Nam sat beside Jin-Dee, resting his head on Jin-Dee's shoulder. Jin-Dee watched Taye's chest rise and fall. He stared at Taye's fingers in his mouth as he slept, the dark daisy-tipped lashes, the healing scratches on his peaches and cream face. Jin-Dee was aflame. He wanted to hold Taye, gaze at him, then mate with him for endless moonrises. Is this how others feel about us? He had never pondered how others perceived him. The ones that were obsessed with him back in captivity. The ones that claimed to love him, want him, need him. The ones that whispered "Jin-Dee" softly in their sleep even as he mated with Nam.

Jin-Dee loved Nam, his 'Moon-ah'. The part of Nam that wanted to possess, protect, and penetrate him. The Nam that pushed him back on their bonded bed, ravaged him, left him panting and breathless, wanting more. Jin-Dee wanted to be Taye's Nam. He wanted Taye writhing beneath him in pleasure, his head back, mouth open in ecstasy as he and Jin-Dee mated and Taye peaked.

He thought back to the first time he mated with Nam, his first time ever. The quiet knock on his dorm room door. Nam standing outside, shirtless, then in the room, his lips against Jin-Dee's, hands in his hair then down his pants. He almost reached his peak at that moment. "Moon - ah. Do not stop," he'd panted. Nothing about his love for Nam diminished his desire for Taye.

When Taye awakened, Jin-Dee and Nam flew him to the shower and showed him how to use it. The shower was located high in the tree, suspended in a knot with an opening to the outside. Rainwater and dew filled the buckets, several large ones, and several medium ones. The buckets were on hinges and had strings hanging down to the wooden platform carved out below.

"Here we are. Now Taye, you pull the string on a medium bucket to get wet," Jin-Dee said.

Taye pulled the bucket and laughed in shock at the cold water on his body. "Jin-Dee help Taye wash?" he asked, putting his fist to his mouth.

"Oh. Cool. Okay." Jin-Dee soaped Taye's body and washed him down with a flower petal, then stood back as the water from the large bucket rinsed the soap from Taye, water droplets catching in his lashes, making them tangle.

Nam stood on the platform with a dry towel watching, his emotions stirred by Jin-Dee's interactions with Taye. We feel it again. Jealousy. We should not be jealous. We are free to mate with any fairy in the hive. And didn't he want to mate with Taye as well? What was going on with him? Nam had fought a macrocosm of talented, world-class performing fairies to win Jin-Dee as his bonded mate. Now, there was a new competitor for Jin-Dee's love and affection. Another chance for Nam to lose his universe, beautiful Jin-Dee.

Or, for Jin-Dee to pay him back for mating with Nightingale, out of frustration, before he mated with Jin-Dee. And there was the time in the recent past when he and Nightingale had spent a full season of a rotation together, mating nightly, without their bonded companions. Just runaway sexual desire, satisfied loudly, over, and over. Taye might be the price for that affair, though it was sanctioned at the time. Yes. Lovers still manage to exact payment, even though no sin has been committed. Lovers have a way of balancing the scales, Nam thought.

"Oh!" Taye said as his arousal became apparent. His eyes wide.

"Taye, that is natural. It is an erection. You will be erect until you reach your peak or are no longer aroused," Jin-Dee smiled at him. "Do you want Jin-Dee or Nam to kiss it?"

"No. Taye is scared of that," he said, shaking his head.

"Oh. Cool. Okay." He patted Taye's wet shoulder. "Do you want to watch me kiss Nam's erection?"

Taye gave a slow hesitant nod.

Nam was aroused and Jin-Dee could feel it. Nam had been aroused since he watched Jin-Dee wash Taye's body with his soft hands while cooing at him affectionately, singing Korean lullabies. Nam dropped the towel and rushed to Jin-Dee, kissed him full on the lips, his hand on Jin-Dee's neck to hold the kiss tighter. Jin-Dee knelt before him, sliding down Nam's pants as he lowered himself to the floor of the shower. Jin-Dee looked up into Nam's eyes as he took Nam's manhood in his mouth.

Taye stared. Transfixed. The heat of the moment traveling to his consciousness, then through his body down to his own arousal. He backed against the wall of the shower, closed his eyes, put one fist to his mouth, and gripped his bangs with the other hand. "Ah. . . ah . . . ah." The pressure built, slow, hard, and insistent in his erection. "Eeeeyeee," he whispered, arched his back against the wall of the shower, and convulsed as he reached his peak in sync with Nam. Nam's head was back, eyes staring up, unseeing, fingers clutching Jin-Dee's wild purple mane.

"Gah," he exclaimed and released into Jin-Dee's mouth, breathless.

Jin-Dee stood, kissed Nam, and hugged him. He turned to look at Taye. “See. Do not be scared. It is only pleasure. No pain.” He retrieved the towel, wrapped Taye in it and brought him close. Taye rested his head on Jin-Dee’s shoulder, eyes closed. “You will mate when you are ready,” Jin-Dee whispered.

That afternoon Nam spent some time showing Taye how to weave blankets and Jin-Dee taught him how to make medicinal herbs. Whenever Taye made a mistake, tears would spring to his eyes, and he would suck his middle and pointer fingers in frustration.

“Do not cry,” Nam and Jin-Dee said as they wiped away the tears.

Jin-Dee could not remember the last time he had cried, or any of the fairies in the hive for that matter. They had been stoic, for the most part, out of habit and training. But instead of being frustrated by Taye’s frequent crying, his tears triggered feelings of protectiveness, not just in Nam and Jin-Dee. Everyone petted and soothed Taye each time tears rose to his eyes, clung to the daisy lashes then splashed onto his cheeks. Often, his tears would resolve to giggles from the attention he received. Taye cried less and less as he acclimated to the hive, a fact the hive found somewhat disappointing, as his tears were an excellent excuse to hold, kiss and comfort him.

~

Taye had been at Euphoria for ten moonrises and was healing well, if slowly. He still couldn’t fly or walk for long distances. But the superficial cuts and scrapes had healed fully. His face was scratch-free, sublime, unblemished peaches, and cream. This morning the hive was assembling for the day's chores, and he sat on his sickbed, bored.

“Taye can help. Please?” He bounced on his butt in the bed with pent-up energy. “Please. Taye go outside? Taye can help the fairies of the hive. Please?”

“He has not been out of the tree for many moonrises,” Nightingale said. “He can come with us. We will watch over him.”

Nightingale reached for Honee's hand, then squeezed it. He could feel Honee's emotions shifting. The trepidation, fear, and insecurity. Nightingale still carried an ember of desire for Nam. Everyone knew it. But it only mattered to Honee, and, of course, Jin-Dee but to a lesser degree. Now the specter of Taye's unmoored, unbonded, sexuality made Honee feel threatened in his relationship with Nightingale. For Honee's part, in a world where every fairy is gorgeous, amazing, perfection, someone had to rank last. When imperfections are measured in micrometers, near imperceptible imperfections are, perceptible. Honee was always apprehensive, that of six exquisite fairies, he was the least attractive. His lips were slightly less plump than everyone else's, his eyes a bit closer and his muscles less defined.

Taye's chipped front tooth did not diminish his singular handsome face. It somehow made him seem sweeter, more alluring. He truly did look like an angel. What creature has daisy lashes? Honee thought Nightingale was the most beautiful fairy when compared to Taye. However, he did not think himself more handsome than Taye. All he wanted was to belong to Nightingale, without fear of losing him. Between Nightingale's continued affection for Nam, and the new virgin frontier that Taye presented, Honee wanted to sit on a mushroom bed alone and simply cry. Honee had not cried, or even contemplated it, in several rotations. Even the season he'd slept alone while Nam and Nightingale mated night after endless night, his rest disrupted by the sounds of their emphatic and passionate lovemaking.

Nightingale understood Honee's apprehension. But he also knew Honee had nothing to fear. Nightingale truly loved Honee with every cell of his body and soul. That, along with the season he'd spent gratifying his desire for Nam, had left Nightingale content. Nightingale kissed Honee, smoothed his hair, then pulled his ponytail. "Honee is the sweetest. Saranghae . . . we love you." Dampness pooled in the corners of Honee's eyes as the tears threatened to run down his face.

"Do not cry, Honee, for you will make Nightingale cry," tears tugged at his voice. "Nightingale cannot stop crying for many moonrises when the tears come. You know this. We do not vibe with crying," his voice cracked with emotion.

Honee nodded and put his forehead to Nightingale's. He snuffed back the tears, wiped his nose, and calmed himself.

Nightingale and Honee took Taye under his arms and lifted him out of the tree as they took flight. Taye squinted in the bright sunlight. He'd missed the sun's warmth on his skin. They flew to a blueberry patch and sat him down with two buckets to fill, keeping their eyes on him as they worked. Butterflies lit on his hair and arms, staying with him the entire time he picked berries.

"Shoo. Go away," Taye said. He waved at the butterflies to go elsewhere. They simply rose into the air, then landed on his arms and in his hair anew.

"We have never seen such a thing," Nightingale mused. "He has an unusual vibe with nature, for some reason."

Some strange faerie magic. Honee thought. Butterflies do not seek us out in this manner. He sighed and reassured himself that, at least butterflies are not a bad omen.

After the buckets were filled, Honee and Nightingale took Taye back to the hive. He was filthy with butterfly dust and sticky with blueberry juice.

"Do you want to shower?" Nightingale asked as he looked over the grubby, grimy fairy.

Taye nodded.

"We need a shower too," Honee admitted.

When Honee and Nightingale got Taye situated, they undressed and showered together. Nightingale loved to wash Honee's long locks, then comb out the tangles and braid Honee's magnificent dark blonde hair into a single braid. Honee reveled in the loving attention from his bonded mate.

Taye watched Nightingale gently wash, comb then braid Honee's hair. Their naked bodies glistening with water droplets.

"Oh!" He gasped as his arousal became apparent. "Taye is sorry."

"You do not have to apologize, Angel Eyes. It is natural to be aroused when you see love. Do you want Nightingale or Honee to kiss it better?" Nightingale offered.

Color crept into his cheeks, and he looked down at the floor of the shower. "Taye is shy." He put his fingers in his mouth.

"That is okay, Taye. We vibe with that. One day soon, you will be ready." Nightingale assured as he brought him a dry towel.

Yes, Taye thought as he wrapped himself in the towel. One day. Soon. He smiled weakly at Nightingale fighting tears. One day. Soon. Maybe Jimi will kiss me.

~

After dinner that evening, the fairies lingered in the dining room. The hollow branch had a long wooden table down the center of it and leaves were used for a tablecloth. When the leaves were removed, the table doubled as a performance stage for singing and dancing. Once a week they rehearsed a song from their captivity and tried out new ones they had written. Taye watched the performance in silence. At the conclusion of the show, he said, "Taye has never heard such singing and or seen such dancing. You are extraordinary fairies. Thank you for taking care of ordinary Taye." His voice trembled with feeling.

"Our pleasure," the hive responded.

"And you are far from ordinary, Angel Eyes," Jimi reassured him, taking his hand, and kissing it. "Far."

"Should we tell Taye about our game?" Honee ventured. "Taye is not ready to mate with one of us, but he does not have to be to play."

"Maybe he is not too shy to play. True?" Kookie said.

Taye looked around, confused, but said "You will not hurt Taye. Taye is not afraid to play with the fairies of the hive."

"Oh. Cool. Okay. Let's go to the play bed," Jin-Dee cooed with delight.

Jimi and Kookie took Taye under his arms and they all flew to the highest mushroom in the hideaway. The bed, an inviting nest, was covered in decorative blankets and pillows with a stack of small towels at the head. The fairies sat cross-legged in a circle, Jimi sat to the right of Taye and Kookie sat to the left. Honee sat next to Kookie, and Nightingale sat to his right. Jin-Dee sat next to Jimi and Nam sat to his right next to Nightingale to complete the circle.

“Now we take each other's hands,” Kookie instructed. “Because we are a hive mind, when we touch hands, we can become a hive body and share sensations. Our game is cascading orgasm. We can orgasm by closing our eyes and calling it to us. Jimi is the fastest, so he is first. True?” Kookie said. Everyone laughed. Blushing, Jimi gave Kookie a playful punch on the arm.

“Taye, you will feel everyone’s orgasms as we feel them. Then you will have your own peak, after which we all come together as a hive. But you must keep hold of our hands,” Kookie said. “Do you still want to play?”

“Taye had an orgasm,” he giggled. “Taye likes that. Taye wants to play.” He bounced with excitement and anticipation.

“When you are ready, close your eyes,” Kookie said.

Taye closed his eyes. But couldn't help opening them to look at Jimi. He wasn’t sure why, but he wanted to see Jimi peak. He watched Jimi take a deep breath, watched his body convulse and his head fall to the side, eyes closed as a small groan escaped flushed lips.

Taye felt warm all over, then heat in his crotch as his own arousal began. He saw Kookie blush, and his body stiffen as his orgasm took him. Taye’s eyes slammed shut as the heat of Jimi’s orgasm spread through his body.

“Ah . . . ah. . . Jimi.” Taye moaned. He fell back on the bed convulsing with a spasm of pleasure. Without warning his whole body flushed with heat. He could feel himself blush from head to toe. “Kookie . . . ah. . . ah.” Taye thrashed, raising his hips off the bed, eyes closed, mouth open. “Jin . . . ah . . . ah . . . Dee.” He felt Jin-Dee’s orgasm rush through him and heard Jin-Dee groan. Taye wanted to suck his fingers, but he was in the grip of Honee’s orgasm, Jimi and Kookie’s hands. “Ah . . . ah . . . Sesang-eeee!” Taye gasped, repeating Honee’s shout of bliss. The spasms of gratification growing stronger with each peak. “Ah . . . ah . . . Moon-ah . . . Gah!” Nam’s orgasm ripped through him. He heard Nightingale sigh as he came and felt the torrid sensation of Nightingale’s orgasm in his own arousal. Then Taye arched his back, his manhood on fire, throbbing, stretching itself upwards toward the starless night sky. “Ah . . . ah . . . ah . . . Eeeeyeee.” Taye lay on the bed still gripping Jimi and Kookie’s hands, his chest heaving. He heard the beginning of the hive orgasm start with Jimi’s groan then slowly crescendo into a chorus of ecstasy rising to the heavens, echoing through the hollow tree like angels coming in accord. Unbidden, his back bowed. His body shivered and trembled as he peaked with the chorus.

Jimi and Kookie fell back against his shoulders, one on each side, spent and gasping. Taye was panting like he’d run a five-minute mile. His heart was racing, his pajama pants sticky with the residue of eight dazzling peaks. He curled into the fetal position against Jimi, fingers in his mouth, and fell into a dreamless sleep.

~

Taye woke with a start. He was alone on the play bed curled in Jimi’s arms.

“You are awake, Angel Eyes. We should get you cleaned up,” Jimi said. He reached by the pillows and produced a damp rag. Jimi helped Taye out of his pajama pants. Then Taye watched as Jimi cleaned the residue of the peaks from his manhood with gentle hands. He sat up, dazed, and looked around.

“Where are the other fairies?” Taye asked.

“They left us alone,” Jimi replied.

Taye looked at Jimi and touched his lips. He felt safe with Jimi. "Jimi will kiss Taye?" He stared at Jimi's lips as he whispered the request.

Jimi moved so that he sat crotch to crotch with Taye. He looked into Taye's eyes then kissed him softly. Jimi felt Taye's small hands in his hair as Taye returned the gentle kiss forcefully. Their twin arousals throbbing together. Jimi took Taye's lips in a long, deep, searching kiss. He felt Taye's hands all over his back, then down his pajama pants. Taye lay back on the bed and pulled Jimi on top of his body. He kissed and bit Jimi's neck until he left a love mark.

"Taye is not scared now. Taye wants to be with Jimi. Jimi will mate with Taye?"

"Yes. As much as Taye desires," Jimi said as he took Taye in another searching kiss. "As often as Taye wants."

~

In the mid-morning sunlight, Jin-Dee and Taye sat alone on the sickbed. The hollow tree, empty of its usual occupants. Jin-Dee held a bowl of medicinal ointment, and his brow was knit in concentration. Taye sat facing away from Jin-Dee, his wings unfurled as Jin-Dee traced the mending wounds in medicinal ointment. "Your wings are almost healed," Jin-Dee said to the back of Taye's head as he worked. You should be flying in a few short moonrises." He patted Taye on the shoulder.

"Jin-Dee-ah will tell Taye what it is like to be bonded?" Taye asked.

"Oh. Cool. Okay. When you are bonded, there is no longer 'me, I, or mine.' There is only 'we, us, ours.' Your bonded mate is your soul, breath, and life. Your bonded mate is your moon, your stars, your galaxy. You are bonded together in one love, dreaming in the same dream."

"Taye likes that," he said as he turned to face Jin-Dee. "Where is Moon-ah?"

Jin-Dee blushed at Taye's use of his pet name for Nam. "How does Taye know we call Nam, Moon-ah? We only whisper it in his ear. . ."

"When you reach your peak," Taye finished the sentence.

“Yes.” Jin-Dee felt his desire catch fire. Felt unbidden ardor rising. He hid his blushing face behind his hands, but he could not hide his arousal.

“Does Jin-Dee-ah want to mate with Taye?” He placed his faerie hands-on Jin-Dee’s and pulled them gently away from his face and stared into his moonstone eyes.

Jin-Dee lunged forward and took Taye’s lips in a fervid kiss and Taye responded with the same intensity and passion, opening his legs, and wrapping them around Jin-Dee in anticipation.

“Yes. We want to mate with Taye,” Jin-Dee said, kissing his lips, then moving down to bite his neck, licking a path from Taye’s shoulder bone, up to his ear, biting, then smelling his hair, freshly washed with flower shampoo. His handheld the back of Taye’s head and felt the baby soft tresses. He stared into Taye’s night-sky eyes and swore he saw stars in them. He traced Taye’s lips with his fingers, then pushed him back on the bed, climbed on top of him, and ground their erections together, both arousals leaking pearlescent liquid. “Yes. We. Want. Taye.” Jin-Dee grunted. He didn’t want to take the time to undress himself or Taye, but he longed for the velvety feel of Taye’s skin under his fingers. He stripped off Taye’s pajamas, then his own clothing without losing eye contact with Taye for a second. “What Taye does to Jin-Dee is wicked. Wicked,” he said again, as Taye bit and sucked his neck, succumbing to raging passion as they rode the wave to completion together.

~

Outside the hive, in a field of sunflowers, Jimi held Nam in his arms and gently rocked him back and forth, stroked his green buzz cut, and sang to him, the familiar lullabies of their childhoods. Nam remembered the last time he cried like it was yesterday. It was the day before Jin-Dee said ‘Saranghae . . . we love you’ and every day before that.

“You know Jin-Dee loves only you, Nam.” Jimi said.

“Yes. We know,” Nam managed to grate out, despite his heaving chest. “But it does not make this better.” He let the tears flow, sobs carried on the wind, up to the cerulean sky and out to the milky way.

~

The hive was not sure which was the greater disruption, Taye's sexual inexperience when he arrived or his new insatiable appetite for mating. After dinner each night he whispered in a different fairy's ear, "Mate with Taye, tonight?"

Nightingale was beside himself with joy when he got the invitation. He lay on the bed face to face with Taye caressing his hair, glowing with anticipation.

"Do you know why you are called Angel Eyes?" he asked Taye, as he touched his hair, ran his fingers down Taye's nose and fondled his ears.

"Taye does not know," he said, intertwining his fingers with Nightingale's and mirroring his touches.

"Because" Nightingale said as he pulled Taye on top of himself, wrapped his legs around Taye's waist and took him in a passionate kiss, "you see from the eyes of one who came from heaven."

~

Honee was apprehensive about mating with Taye, even though he wondered what it would be like to feel Taye pull his ponytail. He sat beside Taye on the sick bed and held his tiny hands.

"Honee is afraid to kiss Taye?" Taye said as he wrapped his arms around Honee. "Taye wants to kiss Honee."

"Honee did not want to be jealous of Taye. Taye is singular. Honee is sorry." He studied the end of his ponytail.

"Taye likes Honee. He is handsome. Honee is the sweetest."

Honee felt tears forming in his eyes when he heard Taye repeat Nightingale's love declaration. He is part of the hive for Taye hears our thoughts. But Honee quickly brushed the tears away. He reached out and ran his thumb over Taye's daisy lashes.

Taye kissed his lips. Then moved smoothly down Honee's neck, taking it roughly in his mouth, biting it, leaving his vampiric love hickey. Honee closed his eyes against the wonderful pain. "Honee will mate with Taye?" Taye said when he pulled back.

Without answering Honee pushed Taye onto the bed and returned his kisses and caresses. He left his own love mark on Taye's neck as he peaked, his ponytail wrapped around Taye's ankle, pulling against the violence of their shuddering orgasms.

~

Taye lay in Kookie's arms, panting and spent. He wanted to suck his fingers, but he wanted to ask a question more. When he regained his breath, he said, "Taye feels Jimi when he kisses Kookie. Kookie will tell Taye what it is like to be bonded to Jimi?"

Kookie took a deep breath. "It is like being one soul in two bodies. It is like being wrapped in a warm blanket against the bitter cold. It is like having his name written in fire on our heart, ever burning. But it is also being afraid every day that something will take him away."

"Kookie is afraid that Taye will take Jimi away?"

Kookie looked deep into Taye's night-sky eyes. "Never. Taye is part of the hive now."

~

Nam lay on the bed curled in the fetal position; eyes full of tears that refused to spill onto his cheeks. Jin-Dee sat, legs crossed beside him, caressing his green buzz cut. Taye sat legs crossed, beside Jin-Dee, head on his shoulder, hand on Jin-Dee's knee. Taye's other hand was curled in a tight fist against his lips.

"We want to mate with Taye, but we cannot." Nam closed his eyes and let the tears fall.

"Taye make Moon-ah cry?" Taye asked.

"No, Jin-Dee makes Moon-ah cry. Love makes Moon-ah cry," Jin-Dee said. "Nam feels Jin-Dee's love in his soul, but not in his body. He will be okay when his soul and body rejoin."

~

That evening, the fairies sat at the dinner table set with bowls of steaming wild rice, blueberries, flower buds, and honey wine. Tonight, was a celebration. Taye's wings and right foot were finally healed. Jimi held up a glass of wine in toast.

"To Taye becoming part of Euphoria," Jimi said, and everyone cheered.

"Thank you," he said. "Taye likes that. Taye is grateful for all the fairies of the hive did to help him get better. That the fairies mated with Taye." He studied his hands for a few minutes, daisy lashed eyes downcast then added, "Taye wants to be bonded."

All breathing stopped and anxious anticipation filled the room. What will Taye say next? Who would be a throuple? Who might he break up? Nam looked down and saw that tears were falling onto his hands.

"Taye wants his own bond. Taye wants," he paused then added sheepishly, "a girl."

~

When the moon cleared the tree line this night, it shone down on Euphoria, now with seven fairy occupants, reconciled and peaceful. Taye slept alone in his own bed created for him by the fairies of the hive. He curled under a woven blanket shaped like a butterfly made for him by Nam and Jin-Dee. His head rested on down filled pillows stuffed by Nightingale and Honee. He wore pajamas sewn by Jimi and Kookie with the name "Angel Eyes" embroidered over his heart. His hand was curled in a small fist next to his lips and he dreamed about his own bonded mate, a girl to dream in the dream with him. Her name in fire, burning in his heart.

Below him, Jimi spooned with Kookie.

"Sleep tight, Kookie our love," Jimi whispered.

"Sleep tight, Jimi our love, and do not let the Angel Eyes bite,"

Kookie said, making Jimi snicker.

On the mushroom bed they shared, Honee hugged Nightingale close. "Nightingale is the most beautiful fairy in the world," Honee said and kissed Nightingale's ear.

"And Honee is the sweetest," Nightingale said, his wrist wrapped tightly in Honee's ponytail.

As the clouds shadowing the moon's penumbra turned from gentle red to bright white, Jin-Dee and Nam cuddled on their bonded bed.

"Jin-Dee is the fairest of them all," Nam said softly, as he lay face to face with Jin-Dee, touched his lips and looked into his eyes.

Jin-Dee gently took Nam's fingers, squeezed them, and kissed the tips. "Moon-ah. Saranghae . . . we love you."

Thank you for reading and please leave a review for our authors!

www.ingramcontent.com/pod-product-compliance
Lightning Source LLC
LaVergne TN
LVHW090124160826
845673LV00015B/836
* 9 7 9 8 8 2 9 3 5 0 6 0 4 *